MISSION LOG 1-13

CODE NAME MASTERPIECE

by Sam Pate and Allison Rose

DORRANCE PUBLISHING CO
EST. 1920
PITTSBURGH, PENNSYLVANIA 15238

Dorrance Publishing Co
585 Alpha Drive
Pittsburgh, PA 15238
Visit our website at *www.dorrancebookstore.com*

ISBN: 978-1-6376-4382-2
eISBN: 978-1-6376-4416-4

MISSION LOG 1-13

CODE NAME MASTERPIECE

DEDICATION

CONTENTS

CHAPTER ONE

Dresden Connors settled down into the uncomfortable desk chair in his cubicle and had barely relaxed when the phone rang. Sighing in annoyance, he picked up the receiver.

"Agent Connors, who am I speaking with?" He was instantly barraged with a deluge of Arabic that took the translator implant in his cell phone a minute to correct before he heard English on the other end. He rolled his eyes as he recognized the tone of the finicky King of Qatar and the absolutely hideous meowing of the white puffball the King called his cat. "Hello, Mr. Hakim—pardon, *King* Hakim, what may I do for you?"

Suddenly, he heard a growl of frustration from across the office. He opened the communications program on his desktop, switching the phone from his hand to his shoulder. Trying to make as little noise as possible to keep the king from launching into an angry speech on the disrespect of 'these westerners,' he shot a quick message to the front desk.

Connors: What are you doing?

"Yes, yes, I'm very sorry. No, we did not mean to track mud on your palace carpet, my apologies. Yes, I will give them a very stern talking to." Connors stifled a chuckle. As the king launched into another angry speech about the colors of oriental carpet and how much it cost to clean, there was a small *ping* from Connors' computer which the king was thankfully too busy screaming to hear.

Neilson: Um? You're supposed to be 'too busy' to talk all the time, mate. Get out of my personal space.

Connors: I'm nowhere near you. And yet, I can still hear you screaming.

Neilson: I'm just working…

Connors: I swear if you're playing space invaders again, I'm going to kill you.

Neilson: I'm not!!!

Connors: …

The king had finally gotten to the heart of the rant: how these 'western Agents' hadn't observed the rules of courtesy of letting the honored guests eat the sheep's eye at the family feast. One of the younger Agents had the nerve to say that it was gross and even spit it out at the table! An insult to all Middle Eastern culture! A disgrace! This must be fixed immediately!

"How terribly rude, I'm awfully sorry, yes, I will take it up with him immediately. Yes, your majesty, I know how important your support is to this Agency. Yes…"

Neilson: …it's The Sims.

Connors let out a chuckle before promptly covering his mouth. He paused a moment, wondering if the king had heard him over his yelling. Thankfully, he had not.

Neilson: Hey, I heard that.

Connors: Shouldn't you be working?

Neilson: Shouldn't you?

Connors: I am working

Neilson: On what exactly?

Connors: I'm on the phone with King Carpet over here and his cat. You know, that cat is almost as annoying as you.

Neilson: Wait, what kind of carpet? Not more of that blasted ancient stuff! That's so out of style; I need a calculator to find out when it was in. Tell him to go to Bed Bath and Beyond or somewhere.

Connors: I don't think they have one of those there.

Suddenly, an email notification popped up in the corner of his screen.

"Your Majesty, I'm going to have to call you back." Dresden hung up the phone before the king could yell at him and promptly stood up and walked out of his cubicle, leaving the notification up on his computer.

The Director requests your presence in his office.

•   •   •

BAM. A gunshot. BAM BAMBAM. Three more.

Jordan O'Connell reloaded her weapon.

"Not bad." The girl next to her nodded, holding a clipboard. "Nearly a perfect score. If you don't miss any in the next clip—"

"I don't miss." Jordan loaded another clip into her pistol.

"Chill out, tough stuff. Your evaluation isn't for another week. You can afford to ease up just a bit," the girl teased.

Jordan paused and turned to her partner. "I really want to pass this evaluation, Daisy."

"Don't worry, you will. You far exceed the requirements. We've had five missions in the past month. That's more than any other duo in the whole Agency." Daisy leaned against the wall of the shooting range.

"But not more than the Agents without partners," Jordan muttered.

"What's that supposed to mean?" Daisy set the clipboard on the counter amongst the empty clips Jordan had already used.

Jordan looked her partner up and down, her eyes briefly scanning over her brown cowboy boots, up past her teal leggings and purple t-shirt, all the way up to her face with its Asian complexion and her long black hair that flowed past her shoulders. Her partner had always made her feel very dull, as she wore her black leather combat boots with her dark jeans and black t-shirt. They had been partners for nearly two years, after what had happened with Jordan's last partner. Jordan shook her head, shaking the thought loose.

"Nothing, I'm just stressing out about this evaluation." Jordan cocked her pistol and aimed at the target sheet that she hadn't bothered to switch out. It didn't matter anyway; her bullet holes were in nearly the same spots every time. She put her finger on the trigger and concentrated, slowing her heart rate as she breathed deeply.

Abruptly, her and her partner's phones beeped in sync with a new email, the sudden noise startling her, causing her to flinch slightly, hitting the target's arm rather than its head. She swore and set the gun down on the table, pulling her phone out of the back pocket of her jeans.

"The Director needs to see us," Daisy read aloud. Jordan nodded, twirling her pistol into her holster and strolling out of the gun range, grabbing her black leather jacket off of the hook and shrugging it on as they walked out the door.

•　　•　　•

Agent Connors stood in front of the Director's desk. He looked into the Director's piercing hazel eyes as he tapped his foot, a nervous tic he had developed. The tall Agent looked up and down the Director's dark complexion, attempting to read him. This didn't work, but he thought he would try anyway.

"What do you need, sir?" Connors forced his foot to stop tapping.

The Director slid a file across his desk. "I have a mission for you."

Dresden swiftly picked up the file and scanned the cover. It was for his rank, all right. He shifted the folder slightly, allowing the light to catch on the silver letters that read *Alpha-Seven*. He had only recently obtained this rank, but he was proud nonetheless. He had reached Silver ranking some time ago, as the first Silver Level was Alpha-Five. Levels One through Four were Bronze ranked, but he was most looking forward to being one step closer to Gold Level. He opened the folder to the first page. "Art theft? That seems easy enough. I'll get right on it." The Agent started to turn toward the door.

"Not so fast." The Director held up his hand, motioning for Connors to stay where he was. Dresden's feet sunk into the ground as if he were standing in quicksand. "This mission requires a partner, and according to my records, you haven't had one in three years."

Dresden stood for a minute and pondered. "Alright, I'll do it. On one condition." The Director raised his eyebrow, as it was rare for an Agent to challenge him. "Adley gets to be my partner."

"Agent Neilson?"

Dresden nodded. "Yes, sir."

"Has he not presently taken over as secretary?"

"He's still a fine Agent, sir. I can keep an eye on him. And he still has the clearance." Dresden did his best to hide his eagerness.

After what seemed like years to Dresden, the Director finally spoke. "Alright, I shall alert Agent Neilson."

"Thank you, sir." Dresden nodded, turning to walk out the door again.

"One more thing," the Director piped up, causing Dresden to wince before he slowly looked over his shoulder with his usual passive smile.

"Yes, sir?"

"This is a dual pair mission."

Dresden turned swiftly, something that would have caused his red hair to fall into his eyes were it not slicked back. "You mean…?"

"Yes Connors, you'll have to work with another pair."

The Director waved an airy hand toward the doorway that Dresden had been so eager to leave through, and Jordan strolled into the office, her hands respectfully clasped behind her and her posture straight enough to balance a teacup on the top of her head. Daisy bounced in behind her, having to walk very swiftly to keep up with Jordan, who walked faster due to her long legs.

"You requested to see us, sir?" Jordan nodded respectfully to the Director. It was only then that she turned her head slightly to acknowledge the other person in the room. Jordan's eyes swept over him, instantly making a dozen deductions.

He was tall, a few inches taller than Jordan, probably around six-foot-three, and he was skinny but didn't look fragile. His black work shoes glistened from a recent shine, and his brown slacks crumpled from sitting in a chair for too long. He wore a brown jacket with black sunglasses sticking slightly out of the pocket, indicating he had recently gotten back from a trip, as it had been raining here for the past two days. However, the Agent's natural light brown complexion hadn't burned, so his visit must have been short.

His wristwatch was set ten hours ahead, so his trip must have been far away. She mentally flicked through the countries in that time zone, among which was Qatar. She had heard about a mission there that had just taken place, in which one of the new Silver Agents had monumentally screwed up by offending the king. This is why they didn't allow Bronze Level Agents to go overseas.

The man's head leaned slightly sideways naturally as if he were used to holding something to his shoulder with his chin, most likely his phone. He had red hair so vibrant it looked as if his head were about to catch fire, that was slicked back so that not a hair was out of place, and he had a light dusting of freckles on his cheeks. He wasn't looking at Jordan, but even from where she was standing, she could tell that he had shocking blue-green eyes, and he held his gentleman's cane with the golden globe symbol on the Agency on the top of it. The official name of the Agency was The International Cooperative Agency, but most people just referred to it as 'The Agency'.

Overall, he looked to be a few years older than her, probably around twenty-five judging by his features.

After she was satisfied with her deductions, her eyes met the Director's again.

"Yes, I have an assignment for the two of you." The Director slid them each a mission file. Jordan took both of them off the desk and handed one to Daisy, who immediately looked at the cover.

"Um, sir?" Daisy asked quietly.

"Yes, Agent Muhuaná?" Daisy smiled when the Director pronounced her last name right, as people could rarely pronounce the Chinese. Her given name was Daijeé, but she started going by Daisy when she moved to the states from the province of Shandong, where she was born.

"I, I'm only Alpha-Five, I don't have the clearance for this mission yet." Daisy looked at the ground sheepishly.

"I'm aware, Agent Muhuaná, but your partner does, so I am granting you temporary clearance, just for this mission."

"Thank you, sir," Daisy said gratefully.

"Why the lower rank? I'm Alpha-Eight," Jordan inquired. Dresden rolled his eyes.

"Agent Connors is an Alpha-Seven," the Director explained.

"Wait, this is a dual pair mission? Is that why he's here?" Jordan gestured toward Dresden, who looked at her for the first time since they had entered. His eyes danced around her pale complexion, and she crossed her arms over her chest defensively, her straight posture and perfect stillness giving him nothing to read, a skill she had refined over the years during undercover ops.

"All due respect, sir, but do we really need four Agents for this mission? I'm sure that one pair can recover something as simple as this…" Dresden knew better than to argue with the Director, but he was not looking forward to having to work with the condescending Senior Agent.

"Ordinarily, yes, Agent Connors. The painting itself is a simple Revolutionary War painting. However, we have reason to believe that the people behind this theft have a larger end goal in mind, and could perhaps be a part of something bigger. I want you four to investigate."

"Yes, sir." Jordan nodded, her gaze leaving the other Agent and moving back to the front of the room.

"The reason I have paired you up is because I believe this mission requires special skills which you all possess." He pointed to Daisy. "Agent Muhuaná is tech, Alpha-Five, and Agent O'Connell is a skilled combatant, as well as a threat assessment operative, Alpha-Eight."

Jordan extended her hand for Dresden, who took it. Jordan shook his hand firmly, a sign of dominance, as he attempted to do the same. Connors pulled away first, balling his hand into a fist, and Daisy suspected he was checking to make sure he didn't have any broken fingers.

"And Agent Connors is combat and strategy, Alpha-Seven."

"So, Seven, where's your partner?" she asked, tilting her head condescendingly.

Dresden sighed. This was going to be a long mission.

•　　　•　　　•

Dresden sat in his cubicle before the others could arrive to work on the case. "Mission Log One Dash One, Mission Code Name Masterpiece, February Fourth, Thirteen hundred oh-seven hours, Agent Dresden Connors. Agent Neilson and I have been paired with two young Agents in order to solve this case. One of which isn't even the correct rank. Honestly, I am unsure of what these two bring to the table. However, this mission seems easy enough, so, with any luck, it will be over within the week. This is Agent Dresden Connors, signing off."

CHAPTER TWO

Half an hour after they had left the Director's office, the three of them were crammed into the confines of Dresden's cubicle. Jordan had established herself at Dresden's desk; her combat boot-clad feet planted squarely in the center of his spotless desk. Daisy, perched on the arm of the chair her partner was lounging in, was nervously glancing back and forth from her partner to the auburn-haired man who had his arms crossed over his chest, visibly displeased about the invasion of his already cramped cubicle.

"Have you reviewed the case file?" Dresden tilted his head toward Jordan.

Jordan leaned her head back and looked up at the ceiling, the closest she could get to meeting the eyes of the Agent that stood behind her. "No, Seven, I'm completely incompetent." She rolled her eyes, annoyed. "Of course, I've reviewed the file."

"Where is it then?" Dresden walked to Jordan's chair and loomed over her.

"My cubicle."

"Didn't you bring it with you while you were making yourself at home?" The Agent's voice had a slight edge to it.

"I already memorized it," Jordan said breezily, shrugging. "Did you expect me to come to a meeting unprepared, Seven?"

Dresden wrinkled his nose in disgust, quickly erasing the gesture and returning to a mask of efficiency. "I'm surprised that you could memorize that much information in such a short time, O'Connell."

Daisy immediately stood from the chair as Jordan shoved a foot against the desk, causing the chair to spin around erratically, slowing to a stop in front of Dresden, meeting the curious colored eyes of the tall man. "And I'm surprised that a Silver

Level Agent wouldn't bother to read the files of the Agents he has been assigned to work a case with, Connors," she retorted. "If you had, you would know I have an eidetic memory."

Dresden stiffened, his hands clenching tighter around the globe on the top of his cane. "Well, since you've *memorized* the file, can you review the basics of the case for us?" the Agent asked through gritted teeth.

Jordan sighed. "Since you haven't done your research, I suppose I will have to do the Mission Log for today. I'll do that before I leave," she muttered to herself, whirling back around in the chair, and Daisy once again perched on the arm of it. She turned on Dresden's desktop and placed Daisy's bright pink laptop on the desk, turning it toward Daisy, so she had access to it. Daisy immediately started typing, her fingers a blur on the keyboard. "So, Connors, when is your partner going to get here? He seems to be awfully late," Jordan asked.

Dresden ran his fingers through his red hair and idly pulled his phone out of his pocket. "I have no idea what's taking him so long. He said he'd be here about five minutes ago." The Agent shook his head, and Jordan could have sworn she heard a note of concern in his voice.

Jordan gave him a hard stare, flicking her gaze back over to the door. "We're a bit pressed for time here. The painting has already been gone for nearly twenty-four hours. I say we should start without him."

Daisy, who had been silent for a good majority of the time, nodded. "I have some super cool tracking technology I want to try out on this mission," she commented enthusiastically.

Dresden frowned, a single line dipping down in between his eyes expressing his displeasure. "As much as we both dislike the assignment, the Director explicitly stated that this was a *dual pair* mission, and we're missing twenty-five percent of our team at the moment. I say we wait for Agent Neilson."

Jordan got up out of the chair, lifting her chin to amend for the small height difference. "Now Connors, who's the highest rank here?" she challenged.

Dresden straightened up, and the air was becoming incredibly tense when there was a slight breeze as someone practically flounced into the room. "Hallo, did someone mention me?" The less than punctual Neilson beamed.

The taller Agent turned his back to Jordan and addressed his partner. "You're more than five minutes late to a crucial mission meeting, Adley. Did you get caught up critiquing desk organization again?"

His partner stuck out his bottom lip in a pout. "No, it was Miss Tralala or whatever her name is. She was being demanding and wearing a couch cover."

Jordan snorted in spite of herself, quickly disguising it as a cough. She instantly turned her attention to reading this new arrival.

Jordan noticed his voice before his appearance. He had an American accent, but what intrigued Jordan were the remnants of a native Estonian accent, as well as a hint of a residential French one. She suspected he was born in Estonia and lived in France for about a year, probably in college.

After she had satisfied herself with this information, she then allowed her eyes to flow over him, observing his physicalities. He had a small goatee that was impeccably groomed, large brown eyes that filled a good portion of his face, a Frenchman's mustache, and his clothes reminded her of a fashion ad she had seen recently on the news. He looked to be about half a foot shorter than his partner.

His blond hair was up in a ponytail that seemed to have a life of its own, and went surprisingly well with the very narrowly yellow-lined purple suit coat he was wearing, sporting a daffodil in the buttonhole that matched the pale yellow, equally narrow pink-lined high-collared shirt underneath the jacket. Complete the suit with dark khakis, and it created quite a bold statement. On anyone else, it would have made them look like a clown, but somehow, the slightly plump posh Agent pulled off the style like it was a red-carpet debut.

When he noticed her scrutiny, he turned around and gave her a beaming smile and a cheery little wave before turning back around to his partner who was reprimanding him for 'negligence to the Agency', or some other embellished grievance.

She interrupted the partners' banter with a clearing of her throat. "We need to focus on this art theft, not the fashion section of the *New York Times*," she pointed out.

Dresden flushed angrily, but Adley merely shrugged, sending his blond ponytail swishing softly around his face. "Of course, darling. Where shall we—" he froze, staring in horror at the far end of the cubicle where Daisy was typing away on her computer.

Jordan followed his gaze, her hands clenching into fists. "What? What about Daisy?"

Adley closed his eyes and gave off a long sigh of remorse. "And I thought that Miss Tricycle's outfit was terrible," he groaned.

Daisy looked up from her computer. "Well, not everyone can look like a model," she muttered, crossing her arms in front of her for a moment.

Adley shook his head. "But you're wearing *teal* and *purple*. What thoughts went through your head this morning to make you think that was okay?"

Jordan protectively stepped in between the condescending man and Daisy. "Don't come in here and criticize my partner," she growled, looming over him by a good three inches.

Adley put his hands up in a defensive position. "Sorry, just trying to provide a lesson on aesthetics to the less educated."

Jordan scowled. "Look here, pretty boy; you don't walk in and make *anyone* feel bad, no matter the excuse." She took a step closer. "If you insult her one more time, you will surely regret it," she hissed.

A flinty voice sounded right behind her as she raised a fist. "I assure you, O'Connell, I can offer the same," Dresden said, tapping his stick forcefully on the ground between Jordan's feet.

She lowered her arm, still shooting Adley a dangerous glance. "Leave her alone, or your fancy jacket is going to turn quite an ugly shade of brown," she threatened.

"Technically, red mixing with this violet would turn my suit jacket maroon, but that's beside the point. And I don't think I would be talking Ms. Black-on-black." The shorter man looked Jordan up and down, judging her outfit.

For a split second, a murderous look flashed in Jordan's eyes, before she took a deep breath and relaxed her hands by her sides. "Can we just get to work please?"

The two men looked at each other, then shrugged simultaneously.

"Daisy thinks she can track the stolen painting by checking the security feeds," Jordan began.

"Actually," Daisy interrupted, gaining everyone's attention. "Whoever took the painting was smart enough to disable the security cameras, so I've resorted to checking the traffic cameras outside of the building. The exterior cameras of the museum run using the same system as the interior ones, so disabling the system rendered all of them temporarily useless. However, if I can make my way into the red-light camera across the street…" Daisy trailed off, typing furiously on her laptop. "Perfect. Look, there's a white van leaving the crime scene. The van has no plates because that's not suspicious at *all.*" The small girl giggled. "I can track where the van went using the traffic cameras around town, but it's probably going to take a couple of hours to decrypt all the cameras and sort through everything."

"Perfect, that gives me time to get some more training in." Jordan grinned.

"Dres, quick question," Adley began, not paying attention to what Daisy or Jordan was saying.

"Oh, here we go," Dresden muttered.

"Why does your desk arrangement look like a rainbow ate one too many scoops of ice cream and was sick all over it?" Adley questioned. "I mean really, a sunburnt orange pencil holder, sky blue file folders, and what is this pen collection?" He picked up a cup with pens of every color, carefully, as if it had a contagious disease. "Seriously, this makes Daisy's outfit look like Jordan's."

Dresden quickly snatched the cup from Adley, carefully placing it back on the desk, adjusting it so it was perfectly straight just like everything else in his cubicle. "The reason I have so many desk accessories is that you always throw out perfectly good ones! I mean really, who throws out unused pens! You can't let those go to waste! Do you have any idea how much paperwork I have to fill out every mission? Do you have *any idea* how many pens I go through?"

"Someone has to warn the Director, I'm afraid he's going to look directly at your paperwork and have a seizure due to all of the colors," Adley joked.

Suddenly, a loud whistle reverberated off the walls of the small cubicle. The three of them looked at Jordan, who had her fingers raised to her mouth.

"Can we focus, please?" Jordan asked, annoyed. "I swear you two fight like an old married couple," she muttered. She turned to talk to Daisy and was too busy looking at her computer screen to notice Dresden's face had turned nearly as red as his hair.

"Right, yes, of course. Adley, we should go get some training done as well, it's been awhile since you've seen combat." Dresden nodded toward his partner, hastily walking out of the cubicle only to reappear in the doorway a few seconds later. "Don't touch anything," he added before disappearing again with Adley in tow.

"Whatever you say, Seven," Jordan muttered, slowly rising out of the chair and tilting her head as a satisfying pop emitted from either side of her neck. She interlocked her fingers and stretched her arms out in front of her, several cracks escaping from her fingers. She sighed.

"They seem nice." Daisy looked up at Jordan and smiled, reminding her of a small puppy.

Jordan shook her head and smiled genuinely for the first time since this mission was assigned. "You're adorable." She patted her partner on the head, turning to walk out of the small cubicle and stretch her legs a bit.

"Do you disagree?" Daisy asked after her.

Jordan stopped in her tracks, thinking for a moment. She spoke without turning to face Daisy. "No, I don't. The tall one seems especially interesting." She smiled to herself before walking out, leaving Daisy to her work.

•　　　•　　　•

Jordan strolled into her cubicle and sat down in her chair, releasing a shaky breath. She leaned forward and pulled out the hair band that held her ponytail in place, running her fingers through her long blonde hair, a clear sign that she was stressed out. The tall woman squeezed her eyes shut for a moment before letting out a sigh and tying her hair back again. She looked at her watch, pressing one of many buttons on the side as a small microphone popped out of the device.

"Mission Log One Dash Two, Mission Code Name Masterpiece, February Fourth, Fourteen hundred seventeen hours, Agent Jordan O'Connell. Agent Muhuaná believes she can locate the stolen painting by tracking the van that was seen leaving the scene of the crime. According to my research, Agent Neilson has been out of the field for three years and might be a bit rusty, however, most of his file was classified for Gold Level Agents only, which also leads me to be suspicious. Agent Connors has taken to helping Agent Neilson prepare for combat, as it has apparently been some time since he has been out of a secretarial position. Agent Connors seems uneasy about working with others; I feel as if he may be hiding something. Agent Neilson also seems a bit uncomfortable. However, I don't believe his problem lies in working with others, rather being back in the field. I will have to keep an eye on him to make sure he can take care of himself. I was unable to find out what rank he was, as that part of his file was also classified. This is Agent Jordan O'Connell, signing off."

She pressed the button again, the microphone snapping back into the sleek watch, and she knew that the Mission Log would be automatically uploading to her computer for the Director to access later if he wished to check in on their progress.

Jordan spun in her chair, swiftly getting up and leaving the room, heading toward the training wing.

CHAPTER THREE

Jordan strolled into the Training Wing of the same building, her duffel bag in hand as she walked into one of the many rooms, going through the maze of punching bags before reaching the one she always used. She set her bag down and pulled out a roll of athletic tape, wrapping it around her knuckles and taking a few half-hearted swings at the punching bag before hearing muffled voices coming from a few punching bags over. She picked up her bag and walked toward the sound curiously, only to discover Dresden and Adley sparring together. They made a good pair, Adley seeming to predict where Dresden was going to swing before he even raised his fist, while the red-haired Agent used a variety of different attacks to keep the shorter man on his guard. Jordan thought that it would be fun to spar with the taller Agent. Maybe he would present a challenge.

Maybe.

Adley was on the move again, jumping over a well-placed kick and lightly bopping Dresden on the nose.

"The brave and handsome blond knight smote the fearful dragon!" he crowed, ducking to avoid the punch that came his way. Dresden rolled his eyes at the portly narcissist who was currently doing a victory jig and opened his mouth to say something when sudden laughter made him jump, his fists immediately raising in a fighting stance as he instinctively stood in front of his partner.

Jordan raised her hands in mock surrender, still laughing. "Easy, it's just me."

Dresden, still wary, lowered his fists to his side. "I thought you would be hot on the scent of that painting since you're obviously on the ball for the case."

Jordan shrugged. "To be prepared is half the victory," she quoted lightly, jerking a thumb toward Adley. "Some of us need to prepare themselves more than others," she quipped.

Adley drew himself up to his full—still rather short—height in mock offense. "*Ma olensolvunud!*" he cried, dramatically slamming a fist against his chest in a theatrical manner. "Does the lady insult my honor, calling the valiant knight a fat little *weakling?* I may be stout of stature, but not of spirit! I have vanquished the mighty red dragon of the Agency, and now I must defend my honor too? Such a busy day for this great hero!" He bowed with a flourish. "Madam, care for a spar with this *rasvasiga?* I've no doubt you'll win, but this old man needs to preserve his honor." As his partner sighed in exasperation at the excitable Estonian's dramatics, Jordan had to stifle a laugh. They really were quite a comical pair, and very comfortable around each other as well. Perhaps this mission wouldn't be so bad after all.

But that was the future, and Jordan's mind had already become distracted by Adley's challenge. She was never one to back down from a good spar.

"Well, how could I refuse such a challenge? *Alustagem!*" She grinned, dropping her bag on top of the sparring mat, and reveling in Adley's surprised face.

"You speak Estonian?" Adley arched one eyebrow, looking over at his partner, who arched his own eyebrow, mocking his partner's countenance.

She shrugged. "I know many languages. I've been traveling overseas for the Agency since I reached Silver a few ranks ago."

"Wait, you're an Alpha-Eight?" Adley asked, slightly impressed.

Jordan crossed her arms defensively. "Yeah, what about it?"

"A bit young, aren't you?" Dresden interjected.

"I've been here for nearly five years," Jordan snapped back.

Adley put up a hand to stop Dresden from speaking again. "Apologies for my partner. What I was going to say was the Director has been viewing potential Gold Agents for several open positions, and I'm assuming you're hoping to get the job. Don't worry; they can always use a *tugevtüdruk* in the higher offices, especially one with such a keen eye for detail," he purred.

Dresden rolled his eyes again, seemingly a habit around Adley, and cut in. "You challenged her, now quit the small talk and spar! I'm interested to see how badly you fail."

Adley stuck his tongue out at the redhead but quickly turned his attention back to Jordan, who was impatiently waiting for him to stop chatting, her mind already leaping to the best type of combat to use on the fashion-obsessed Agent. "May the odds be ever in your favor," he lightly quipped, cracking his knuckles.

Jordan didn't allow the blond Agent a minute of preparation before launching into her first attack using one of her favorite martial arts techniques: Jeet Kune Do, which taught the user that simplicity is infinitely better than those dramatic kicks and punches that grace so many movie screens. After careful scrutiny of Adley's preferred style, Jordan began with a direct attack, aiming her fist between the chocolate-like eyes of her challenger. He ducked to avoid her punch and grabbed her upper arm while stealthily snaking his leg around her ankles. She stumbled slightly, but leaned into the momentum of the fall, rolling backward onto the ground and quickly jumping back up to face her opponent again.

The movement startled Neilson, and he instinctively turned to face her, where Jordan's other fist sailed in to connect with his stomach, right where his kidneys were.

Adley's strangled *oof* let Jordan know she had hit her target, and the man sank to his knees. Dresden, watching from a distance, took another step closer, his face fixed into a concerned frown. Jordan felt a twinge of guilt. That had been a somewhat vicious swing, delivered with a perfect angle to a vital organ.

Her pity didn't last long when her face was suddenly enveloped in the smell of feet and sweat as she fell to the mat by a rather dirty trip from her opponent, grunting as she landed on her stomach. Rolling onto her back, she did a kip-up, landing in a crouch facing Neilson. He hurriedly backed up, shooting her an apologetic smile and a hasty wave. Jordan slowly stalked toward him, deciding on a new plan of action seconds before Adley sprang at her. She ducked out of habit, intending to send the Agent flying over her head, but instead felt the Agent's arms loosely snaking around her neck from behind, attempting to drag her to the ground. Her elbow darted back, finding its target in Adley's rather flabby stomach, and he abruptly let go, doubling over in response to the attack. Bouncing back up in a moment, he vaulted into the air, aiming a dropkick at Jordan's throat, which she batted aside with a breezy block combined with an instinctual duck.

He landed hard on the floor, barrel rolling before getting back up, his fists flying up like a puppet controlled by strings. Playing the offensive, Neilson threw out a half-hearted throat punch, which Jordan blocked and returned with considerably more force. Adley, seeing this coming, grabbed her arm millimeters away from his windpipe, twisting her arm back toward her body. She kicked him in the shin, and he dropped her arm. Quickly, before he could catch on, Jordan flew at her opponent, tackling him and pinning his arms to the mat. His eyes fluttered shut, and his breathing became much heavier and more labored. Jordan looked down at her captive with satisfaction.

"Any words of surrender?" she asked playfully as the Agent wheezed, the fight obviously taking a toll on him. He groaned and attempted to roll over.

"I wholeheartedly regret eating the last bite of mannavaht today at lunch," Adley said playfully, shooting his leg up and kicking Jordan in the thigh, squirming to get out of her grasp. He freed himself, but only briefly. Jordan's arm came down and put him in a chokehold. He spluttered for a moment, then became limp. Jordan, knowing the age-old trick of false submission, tightened her hold. The Estonian coughed violently.

"Ay! Alright, I know when I'm beat, now let me go!"

Jordan complied, unceremoniously dumping Adley onto the carpet, where he bounced right back up.

"Splendid, spectacular, fantastic! Five of five stars! Darling, you're a regular James Bond! An excellent display and much appreciated." Jordan rolled her eyes, but Dresden noticed the slight blush that was easy to spot against her pale complexion. Ponytail swinging, the enthusiastic Agent turned to his partner. "Dresden, I shall have the remarkable Miss O'Connell tutor me in the art of fighting, for she is your superior!"

The redhead chuckled, a rare sound. "I wouldn't go that far, but she is quite good, isn't she?" Jordan met his gaze and was surprised at the amount of warmth the queer-colored eyes held. Was it toward her? Probably not. She shook her head.

"Perhaps the two of us may settle that another day." Jordan nodded slightly toward the taller Agent, strolling out of the training room with her bag, leaving the other two Agents whispering conspiratorially in her wake.

•   •   •

It had been scarcely ten minutes since Jordan had left the training room and retreated to her cubicle to pour over the case file when a cheerful and familiar voice sounded, drawing her out of her brown study. "Knock knock, special delivery!" Adley announced.

Jordan sighed in exasperation at the blond's antics. "There's no door, come on in," Jordan said rather crossly. She looked up when a shadow fell over the desk. Instead of bubbly Adley, Dresden was back in her office, and he wasn't looking too incredibly happy. Jordan felt herself tensing. "What?" she asked defensively.

The khaki-suited Agent cleared his throat uncomfortably, his almost ocean-teal eyes glancing down at his cane as he twirled it nervously. "Well, ah, since we're unacquainted, and, ah, we have a mission to complete, and minimal work has been done on it—" he stopped short at the odd look on Jordan's face. Dresden sighed and twirled his stick even faster. "Horrible word choice. Terrible start. Not good enough, stepping on toes." He seemed lost on this track for a moment, wincing at whatever thoughts were going through the mind obscured by his curly red hair.

"Well, what's the question?" Jordan tapped her foot idly against the legs of the desk chair.

The tall Agent swallowed hard. "What I meant is, ah, er, if you would like to come over for dinner tonight to discuss crucial points of the case. Just a business meeting, combined with pleasure," he said in a rush.

Jordan stiffened in her chair, looking Dresden up and down. "Is this a joke?" she asked suspiciously.

He finally looked up from his cane. "Oh, ah, never mind, it was a bit of a stretch, anyway," he commented icily, quickly turning and retreating from the cubicle.

Jordan went back to studying the case file, but somehow the words kept drifting around, the letters forming into fragments of conversation that were wheeling around in her head, paired with the cold stare of Agent Connors. *Terrible start. I wouldn't go that far. I'm interested to see how badly you fail. Weakling. Not good enough.*

She shook her head, attempting to dislodge the negativity from her mind. Aloud, she said, "I know I'm good. I don't need anyone else to tell me that."

Oh really? If nobody sees, then nobody cares, a snide little voice commented from the back of her mind.

Jordan furiously pushed the thought out of her head and stared back down at the file in her lap. She was mad that the tall Agent had forced himself into her head, a feat rarely accomplished by anyone. *Focus. Focus.*

Eventually, she gave up on trying to concentrate and made her way back to the training room to clear her head. Adley's challenge had distracted her from her usual training regimen, and since she couldn't concentrate, she might as well go back to her training.

As she made her way through the training wing toward the punching bags, Jordan heard the sounds of mild swearing from the far end of the room in a part of the wing that she rarely entered, the target practice room. One of the leather dummies was pulled out into the center of the large mostly black room, and a lone figure stood with his back to the door, throwing knives in hand. Jordan looked around before cautiously going to watch. She instantly recognized the swearing as the voice of the taller Agent that she couldn't seem to escape no matter where she went.

Leaning against the doorframe of the small room and noticing Connors' cane, she picked it up and began to twirl it smoothly. She watched as the Agent took one of the knives from the table in front of him and muttered something to himself before hurling the knife as hard as he possibly could out of anger. The knife completely missed the dummy, something that usually would make Jordan chuckle, but instead, she felt a twinge of something, she wasn't sure how to describe it. It was almost as if she felt bad for him.

Dresden picked up another knife, and this time Jordan heard what he was muttering to himself. It seemed to be different variations of the words *stupid, idiot,* and *worthless,* and now Jordan really did feel bad.

"You know," she spoke up from the back of the room, startling the Agent into dropping the blade currently in his hand, the blade only centimeters from slicing open his palm. Jordan's heart skipped a beat, but she didn't let it show. "If you lean into the throw, you'll be a bit more accurate."

"What are you doing here?" Connors asked defensively, leaning down to pick up the knife he had dropped.

Jordan shrugged. "Couldn't focus. Came down here to clear my head."

"You too, huh?" Dresden muttered, placing the knife back down on the table.

"Well, um," Jordan began nervously, setting Dresden's cane back in its place leaning against the door frame. "I didn't mean to be rude earlier. I'm not exactly used to people inviting me places." She didn't meet Dresden's eye. "But, if your invitation is still on the table, I think I could discuss some of the case with you over dinner." Dresden looked slightly down at her in surprise. "All I have at home is Ramen Noodles anyway," she added hastily, chuckling nervously.

Dresden said nothing but nodded intently. He picked up a knife and twirled it, turning toward the target. He glanced back at Jordan before leaning into the throw and releasing the knife from his grip, sending the blade flying into the dummy's arm.

"Not bad," Jordan commented, stepping up to the table next to Dresden and picking up one of the small blades. She spun the knife a few times before sending it flying directly into the dummy's chest. Dresden looked at her with a slight surprise in his eyes before she turned and exited the small room.

•　　•　　•

Daisy was sitting in Dresden's cubicle, pouring over the security footage. It was a relatively easy task, however tedious it may be. Checking the time, she saw it was nearly seventeen hundred hours. The others would be leaving soon. She'd have to stay late today, seeing as they were pressed for time. She knew that Jordan wouldn't be happy about it, she'd want her to go home and get some rest, but this wouldn't take long. She remembered that Jordan had told her to update the mission log when she had any new information.

Pressing the button on the side of her watch, she started recording.

"Mission Log One Dash Three, Mission Code Name Masterpiece, February Fourth, Sixteen hundred fifty-two hours, Agent Daijeé Muhuaná. I believe I am nearly done tracking the van leaving the crime scene. I am going to stay late to finish, and we can depart for the location first thing in the morning to investigate. This is Agent Daijeé Muhuaná, signing off."

CHAPTER FOUR

Jordan stood outside the door of the penthouse apartment for which Dresden had given her the address. She looked at her watch. Nineteen hundred hours on the dot. She had always prided herself on being punctual. She leaned forward and knocked on the door, her bicep brushing against her holster. She had thought about whether or not it was appropriate to keep it on when she was going to someone's home, but she had never left the house without it, as it made her feel more secure. Before she had fully rocked back on her feet, the door swung open, revealing Dresden, wearing the same suit as he wore earlier that day. Jordan was relieved that she hadn't been expected to change; she really wasn't used to getting invited anywhere.

"Ah, um, come in," Dresden fumbled, gesturing for her to come inside.

Jordan nodded, walking inside, looking at the large apartment.

The first thing that she noticed when she stepped foot into the apartment was the tasteful color schemes of each room; next, the intricate twisted steel and calming light fawn and white colors of the furnishings. Barely thumbed through, men's glossy fashion magazines resided on a little wooden coffee table at the foot of a white plush couch in what Jordan guessed was the living room. There was a bowl of floating flowers in the center of this arrangement, the lilac lotus swimming in the water perfectly corresponding to the color of the walls of the spacious room. Art pieces that looked like an interesting mix of modern art and Monet were in places of honor on sections of the pastel walls, and as Jordan breathlessly made her way through the apartment, she could see a definite trend in decor: Everything seemed to match, greatly unlike the colorful arrangement of the redhead's cubicle. The foyer where she had entered was a yellow that matched the shirt that Adley wore that day, and on the light-colored wooden tables were strangely-shaped metal vases filled to the brim with primroses and gardenias, which matched the white carpet that covered practically the whole apartment.

The hallway off of the living room took a sharp turn and opened off into a spacious area where a chandelier hung pride of place from the ceiling, and a pale wood replaced the carpet. Two white doors were jutting out of the mint green wall, and she followed her host through the right-hand door and yet another small hall, this one painted baby blue with various black-and-white pictures of flowers evenly spaced, and a chalkboard filled with loopy cursive centered in the passage.

As Dresden led her back into the same open area where the kitchen, dining room, and living room all flowed together, Jordan's eyes were drawn to the kitchen, half of which was done in white tile, where multiple pots and pans were sitting out on the stove. The majority of the appliances and cooking supplies were on either side of the unusual floor. The other half of the kitchen had been styled to look like a hyper-realistic photograph-like mural of a bustling city street from an aerial view, done in black and white, complete with painted raindrops that surely must drive anyone crazy when they're trying to clean it. From a quick glance, Jordan assumed the meticulously painted scene was a rendition of an American city, most likely New York City. Jordan also noticed two wine glasses recently missing from the rack. Her eyes darted to the other end of the room, where the bathroom door was open just enough for Jordan to notice two towels hanging on the rack, and two toothbrushes sitting in a cup on the counter.

"You never mentioned you have a roommate," Jordan commented as Dresden led her to the dining table, taking three wine glasses from the rack and setting them on the table.

"You are quite observant, aren't you?" Dresden's lips turned slightly upwards in a small smile.

"Was that a compliment?" Jordan arched one eyebrow curiously.

One of the glasses suddenly slipped out of Dresden's grip. Jordan's arm reflexively shot out and caught the glass before it hit the ground.

"No," Dresden said defensively.

Jordan chuckled, setting the glass on the table. "Well, thank you." She looked around. "So, can I meet this roommate of yours?"

"Oh, hallo, darling!" A familiar voice rang like a bell behind her.

Jordan spun around to face Adley, who was wearing an entirely new outfit. The blond Agent now wore a sky blue suit with a white shirt, his tie and pocket square both a navy blue.

"Wait, you two are roommates?" Jordan asked, surprised.

Adley crossed to Dresden's side, grabbing his hand, drawing Jordan's attention to the matching silver engagement bands on both of their left hands.

"Oh, so you two are…" Jordan trailed off.

"Is there a problem?" Dresden asked, defensively.

"No, I just couldn't picture anyone dating you," Jordan teased.

"See, darling? I told you she's alright." Adley looked over at Jordan and winked playfully.

Dresden rolled his eyes. "Hush. Come on, the food's getting cold."

•　　•　　•

Jordan had already cut into her steak when Dresden brought over a bottle of red wine. He poured himself and Adley a glass, but Jordan stopped him from pouring her one.

"No, thanks." She raised her hand.

Adley smirked. "Dah-ling, she's just a child, no wisdom-drink for her yet." He leaned over to her, and dramatically whispered: "Don't worry, it gets better with age, like most things worth waiting for."

Jordan crossed her arms defensively. "I'm not a child. But he is right; I'm not of age yet. I'm only twenty."

"Oh, I didn't mean, ah, I mean, I wasn't trying to—" Dresden fumbled apologetically.

"More for us," Adley chirped, picking up the bottle and pouring more wine into his glass. By the time Dresden had lifted his glass and taken a sip, Adley was already halfway done with his.

Dresden took a deep breath. "I wasn't trying to make fun, honestly. It just slipped my mind."

"It's alright; I get it a lot," Jordan muttered.

"I'm sorry about what I said earlier, about you being young. I, ah, didn't mean to…" Dresden trailed off, running his hand through his red hair. Jordan noticed that he had taken the gel out of his hair, and it now flowed majestically around his face, forming little curls that were wispy like a toddler's hair after a bath. "I think it's rather impressive for you to be such a high rank at such a young age."

Jordan smiled a bit, taking a bite of her steak, her face lighting up. "Wow, this is amazing. You made this?" She looked over at Adley.

"No, I don't cook. That's this one's job." He nudged Dresden with his elbow.

"You cook?" Jordan stifled a chuckle.

"He's the best! I even got him this adorable pink apron as an anniversary present last year…"

Suddenly, Jordan dropped her fork, breaking out into hysterical laughter.

Dresden stared daggers at Adley. "See, this is why I never want to take you anywhere in public. You'll tell embarrassing stories about me for *hours*!"

Adley's eyes sparkled mischievously. "Of course, I could tell Miss Bond what happened to you when the advisor of the Queen challenged you to a baking contest on a plane to Swahili with an in-flight kitchen…" he trailed off, seeing the murderous look from Dresden and the curious one from Jordan.

"Miss Bond?" Jordan questioned.

"He gives everyone dumb little nicknames," Dresden explained.

"What's yours?" Jordan arched one eyebrow.

"I call him Con-Man because he's always the man," Adley said, flipping finger guns and winking at Dresden.

The Agent rolled his eyes and pushed back his chair. "If you two will get back on task, I've made macaroons for mission-planning dessert."

"You *bake* too?"

Dresden straightened up, seemingly growing even taller. "Of course. How can you call yourself a chef if you can't make a dessert other than pre-packaged cookies?"

Jordan paused. "What kind of macaroons?"

"Pineapple, Adley worships them."

"No way." Jordan smiled.

"Yes, I know it's an odd flavor, but you should give them a try."

"Are you kidding?!" Jordan exclaimed. "Pineapple macaroons are my favorite!"

"Your favorite macaroons?" Adley questioned.

"My favorite *anything*, they're amazing! You better have done them justice," she teased.

Adley turned toward his partner. "Decent fashion taste, excellent fighting skills, and a connoisseur of macaroons? I *will* adopt her in less than an hour," he teased.

"We'll see about that," Dresden called from the kitchen, where the scent of baked goods was beginning to waft from the oven.

Jordan rose from her seat and began to clear her plate, which she had cleaned completely in record time.

Dresden took the plate from her, depositing it in the sink before opening the drawer next to the oven. He sighed in frustration. "Adley, where's the oven mitt?"

"I rearranged the kitchen, so all of the towels and oven mitts are organized by color from most to least fashionable in the bottom drawer," the blond called from the couch, where he had already begun lounging.

The redhead rolled his eyes playfully. "You can't even leave my bloody *oven mitts* alone."

Jordan noticed a slight British accent all of a sudden, which she hadn't heard before. She suspected one of Dresden's parents was from England.

"The case file is on the coffee table if you want to get started," Dresden called out over his shoulder as he rifled through the drawer to find the oven mitts.

Jordan walked over to the living area and sat down next to Adley. "So, what are these embarrassing stories you were talking about?" Jordan grinned mischievously.

"Well, there was this one time, back in the good old days of the Dresley prime missions when we took a trip to Peru, and the Con-Man *had* to go first into this horribly dangerous jungle, and he screamed like a little girl because his sunglasses were snatched up by a monkey—"

"What are you two talking about?" Dresden swept back into the room, bearing a plate of macaroons and carefully placing white and baby blue china in the center of the table, to which Adley nodded approval.

"My favorite dessert on an aesthetic platter! Is it a holiday?" he asked playfully, winking at Jordan. In a dramatic undertone, the blond added, "He never makes *me* good desserts." The shorter Agent stuck out his bottom lip in a pout that resembled a small child when he didn't get the toy he wanted.

"Wait, so you two were partners before? I read in your file that you've been out of the field for a few years. What happened?" Jordan asked.

"The Agency apparently has a policy about partners being romantically involved. Dresden was prepared to step out of the field, but I decided if I were the secretary, I would be able to redo the Agency's color scheme. Too much red-black with green-black. The only bad thing is that I have to see Miss Triangle everyday wearing a go-dawful homeless outfit from the '80s she stole from her grandmother."

"Is that why you're a solo Agent now?" Jordan asked Dresden, cautiously taking a macaroon from the plate. She eyed it with suspicion.

Dresden nodded. "The Director's been hounding me for a couple of years to get a new one, but I've refused to work with anyone other than Adley." He put his arm around his partner, his hand resting on the shorter man's shoulder.

"Aw, the Tin Man has a heart after all." Jordan grinned, taking a bite of the macaroon. Her eyes lit up.

"Aren't they scrumptious?" Adley asked, picking up his fourth macaroon from the plate and devouring it in two bites.

"These are amazing," Jordan muttered.

Dresden looked up, surprised. "Really?"

Jordan smiled. "Yeah, they're the best macaroons I've ever had. I don't get them often. I don't really get out much," she muttered, looking down at the half-eaten macaroon in her hand.

"Well, feel free to help yourself to as many as you want," Dresden gestured to the plate sitting on the table. "It might do well for Adley's figure if he were not to eat the entire batch." He nudged his partner in the side.

Adley stuck his tongue out at Dresden. "I am perfectly in shape, I'll have you know."

"Yes, round is indeed a shape," Jordan teased, making Dresden laugh.

Adley looked at Dresden. "I'm disowning her."

"Hey!" Jordan exclaimed, in mock offense, still laughing. Suddenly, Jordan's phone rang. She removed it from her back pocket and looked at the screen. Above the automatic *Accept call*, *Decline call*, and *Trace call* options, a familiar number flashed.

"It's Daisy," she muttered, hastily shoving the last of her macaroon in her mouth before answering. "Daisy? What is it? Everything okay?"

Jordan nodded as Daisy spoke on the other end. "Great work. Okay, I'll let them know. Get some rest now. I'll see you tomorrow." Jordan ended the call and turned to the others. "Daisy tracked the van to some warehouse. We leave to investigate first thing in the morning."

"Do I still have time to do my hair?" Adley asked.

Jordan chuckled. "You'll have to get up early, which means we should all get some rest. Adley, would you like to update the mission log?"

Adley stood as Jordan stood, a traditional gesture of chivalry at which Jordan rolled her eyes. He bowed deeply. "It would be my pleasure, Miss Bond."

"I'll see you guys at the Agency first thing tomorrow. Be sure to bring your gear if you need it." Jordan nodded to the both of them, turning on her heel and walking through the long winding hallways to get back to the front door. The penthouse apartment was so large, normally someone wouldn't be able to find their way back to the door, but because of Jordan's eidetic memory, she found her way out with ease.

Adley turned and stuck his tongue out at Dresden. "Told you she was good."

"I know."

Adley went to press the mission log button on his gold-embellished watch.

"Do you remember how to do a mission log?" Dresden asked teasingly.

Adley glanced at him, pressing the button on the side of his watch. "Mission Log One Dash Four, Mission Code Name Masterpiece, February Fourth, Twenty-one hundred thirty-four hours, Agent Adley Neilson. The fabulous Agent Daisy has tracked the van that stole the painting. Well, I suppose the people driving the van took it. Or perhaps the van is a transformer, you never know. Regardless, we shall leave first thing in the morning to investigate the van at the warehouse to which Daisy has tracked it. Why must it always be a warehouse? It's always a warehouse. Isn't it always a warehouse, Dres?" He nodded toward Dresden.

The taller man flipped his bangs out of his eyes and nodded. "Always a bloody warehouse."

"Anyhoo, we shall investigate tomorrow. This is Agent Adley Neilson, signing off."

Adley looked up at Dresden, who had his arm around him again. He grinned. "Okay, okay, so you do remember." Dresden playfully rolled his eyes.

CHAPTER FIVE

The next morning, Dresden and Adley strolled into Dresden's cubicle, where Jordan and Daisy were already waiting. Jordan had her feet propped up on the table, and Daisy was sitting on top of the desk typing furiously on her laptop. The four of them were wearing their mission attire.

All of the clothing was almost completely black, a dress code of which Jordan approved. Their suits included soft black t-shirts, black leggings for the women and black slacks for the men, and their navy rank-personalized Agent letterman jackets, complete with the insignia of the Agency on the collar. It was a subtle detail, as they didn't necessarily want to advertise that they were part of the Agency if they were going to be on an undercover or covert operation. Jordan had on her black combat boots, as she always did. Daisy had on her usual brown cowboy boots as well. Dresden, however, was wearing a pair of black steel-toed boots, at which Jordan nodded her approval. Adley wore a pair of men's combat boots, rather different than the ones Jordan wore.

"I really hate these shoes," Adley muttered as he walked into the cubicle, staring at his feet with clear disdain as if a cat had emptied his stomach onto them.

"Oh, calm down, you'll be alright. They're more practical than those black leather monstrosities you were trying to find in the closet this morning."

Adley pouted. "But those had *fringe* and were *shiny*. Since when do you care about the way anything looks, anyway?"

"I don't." The taller Agent crossed his arms, a bit of his British accent coming out. "I care about the fact that those boots weigh about ten pounds and would have dragged you down. Plus, have you ever tried to go on a covert op with *fringe* on your shoes? Terribly impractical."

"If you two are finished—" Jordan interrupted the two, standing up from Dresden's chair, "we really should be going."

"I have the location pinned down; it's not far from here. They haven't left town; we still have a chance." Daisy pushed herself off of Dresden's desk, twisting like a cat to land in a crouch on the carpet before turning and grabbing her laptop off the desk.

"Wait, you're bringing that?" Dresden asked.

"Why wouldn't she? She needs it to track where we're going." Jordan said matter-of-factly. "Plus, she's rather attached to it."

"It's hot pink." If Jordan didn't know better, she would have thought she detected a hint of disgust in his voice.

"Don't worry; I got you covered." Daisy grinned, sliding a black laptop cover over the top of her laptop. She looked up at the others expectantly. "Get it? Covered? Because…" she trailed off.

Jordan ruffled her partner's hair.

"Shall we?" Adley spoke up from behind Dresden.

"One second." Jordan pressed the button on the side of her watch. "Mission Log One Dash Five, Mission Code Name Masterpiece, February Fifth, Oh-Six Hundred hours, Agent Jordan O'Connell. The four of us are going to investigate the warehouse to which Agent Muhuaná has tracked the stolen painting. This is Agent Jordan O'Connell, signing off."

"Ready?" Dresden looked at the three of them.

Jordan nodded. "Ready."

•　　•　　•

The four of them walked into the warehouse.

"What exactly are we looking for? It's not like a stolen painting is just going to be sitting around on a chair with a free bottle of wine and a sign that says 'take me,' though I would take the free bottle," Adley commented.

Jordan and Dresden were leading, as they couldn't seem to settle the dispute as to who would stay back. Adley and Daisy were further behind, Daisy carrying her laptop.

"…and Dresden said, 'always a bloody warehouse'! I told him you can't pick your crime scene, and he gave me *the look*, and I was somewhat mortified. Such a terrible *faux pas*." Adley sighed dramatically, causing the shorter girl to smile.

"That's not how it went down at all, and you know it," Dresden called over his shoulder.

Adley winked at Daisy. "Dresden darling, you know me, always trying to impress the ladies."

Dresden rolled his eyes. "Honestly, if I didn't know you were gay, I'd call you Don Juan."

"Oh yeah, Jordan mentioned that. You guys make a cute couple." Daisy giggled.

Suddenly, a small noise sounded throughout the supposedly empty warehouse. Jordan raised her gun so fast she heard it whip through the air, balancing it on her left wrist as her eyes darted around. Dresden looked at her before doing the same. Jordan met Dresden's eye, and she could see that Dresden was slightly nervous. She gave him a reassuring look. "Do you want me to take point?" she asked.

"If you insist." Dresden gestured in front of him, allowing Jordan to step in front of him. As Jordan rounded the corner, she looked back to the others and motioned that it was all clear. As the other three walked into the open, suddenly a bullet shot past Jordan's head.

"Contact!" she yelled, grabbing Adley, who was the closest to her at the time, and ducking behind a small pile of crates. Dresden and Daisy ducked behind a similar stack across the corridor. Bullets continued to fly past them, hitting the boxes and splintering the wood.

Jordan peered around the container, and she saw multiple figures in dark suits and masks. She immediately ducked down again, before several more bullets came flying in her direction. The blonde woman quickly moved behind a different set of crates, shooting one of the figures in the shoulder and one in the leg, intending to injure, but not kill. She stood next to Adley, who continued to crouch behind one of the boxes.

Daisy drew one of her throwing knives, a weapon she far preferred over her gun, from the inside of her jacket and twirled it in her fingers before standing up from behind the crate and throwing it, pinning one of the figures' shirts to the wall with incredible accuracy.

She drew another throwing knife and threw it into the palm of someone who was shooting at Adley, who looked over at her and gave her a nod of thanks before turning back to their assailants.

Jordan looked over at Dresden, who was shooting at the figures with marksmanship to rival her own, his red curls clinging to his forehead with sweat. She looked back over her shoulder as Adley swiftly ducked behind the crate to reload after unloading a magazine toward the enemy Agents.

"I count thirteen hostiles," Jordan spoke into her earpiece. "I've taken out three…" She watched as someone took aim at Dresden and quickly shot the figure.

"Correction, four, Dresden's taken two, Adley's gotten three, and Daisy got one, so there should be three left by my count."

"Wait, I only count two," Daisy's voice echoed in their ears.

"No, there's three, see..." Jordan trailed off. "Where's the third one?!"

Suddenly, Adley cried out. Jordan whipped around and pointed her gun, but instead, she locked eyes with a woman pressing the barrel of her weapon to Adley's temple. "Drop it," the woman demanded sharply.

Jordan's eyes darted every which way, running through a thousand plans in her mind within seconds. None of them would work without risk. She looked over her shoulder, and her gaze fell on Dresden. His gun was lowered slightly, a shocked and helpless look flashing across his face. Jordan's stomach sank with a feeling she had been trained to avoid: sympathy.

She turned back to Adley as the woman pressed the barrel of the pistol further into his temple, Adley's face contorting in pain. "Now!" the woman shouted. Adley gulped but refused to show fear. Jordan winced and held her hands up in surrender. "Put it on the ground," the woman instructed. Dresden and Daisy obeyed immediately, placing their pistols on the concrete floor, but Jordan hesitated. Their assailant jerked Adley in her grip, causing him to inhale sharply.

Glaring daggers at the woman, Jordan slowly bent over and laid the gun on the floor, straightening back up to assume her usual perfect posture, her hands still lifted in surrender.

Another one of the Agents walked over to Jordan and pointed his gun at her. She raised her chin in defiance, swallowing nervously. "Get on the ground," the man instructed. Jordan glared at him. He suddenly kicked her in the back of the knee, causing her to grunt as she collapsed. She landed on her hands and one knee, kneeling with the other, but glared up at the man who had the barrel of his gun trained on her forehead. The third Agent crossed over to Dresden and Daisy and ordered Daisy to put her last throwing knife on the ground. When she didn't respond immediately, the man punched her in the face, blood spitting from her mouth.

"Hey!" Jordan cried, attempting to stand before she was grabbed and forced back onto her knee, the Agent now pressing his gun against the back of her neck. She clenched her hands into fists, digging her short nails into her palms. Jordan watched as Daisy breathed deeply and spat the blood from her mouth, but slowly removed her knife and laid it on the ground.

Jordan felt the barrel of the pistol leave the back of her neck, and she looked up as the man walked around to the front of her. Jordan watched him carefully. Suddenly, her leg swung out from under her, making him fall to the ground. She reached for her gun, but before she could, the sound of a gunshot rang through her ears, and her bicep engulfed with flame. She fell backward, covering her gunshot wound with her hand. She cried out loudly, biting her lip to stop the string of curses that threatened to escape her mouth.

"Jordan!" Daisy cried out, beginning to stand before the Agent who punched her held her back. Daisy thrashed against the man, kicking at him before he smacked her across the face with the barrel of his gun, knocking her back down. He pressed his own gun against her head, and she finally stopped for a moment. Jordan looked down at her fingers to see them soaked in blood before she picked herself up to a kneeling stance again. She glanced over at Daisy as a tear rolled down her partner's cheek. Jordan locked eyes with her, telling her everything was going to be alright.

"Come on; we're ready, let's get out of here!" A fourth Agent entered from the other side of the warehouse. The man holding his gun against Jordan shoved her onto the ground violently, and she quickly rolled over onto her back to look at the Agent. She lifted her chin in defiance again before he kicked her in the ribs. She grunted, instinctively curling up to protect her ribcage from any further damage. The Agent holding Daisy released her, and she fell to the ground as well.

Dresden simply sat there, his arms raised in surrender, frozen with horror as he watched the woman with her gun against Adley's temple. The Agents walked toward the other end of the warehouse, their weapons still trained on Jordan and Daisy. The woman holding Adley met Dresden's eye, her lips spreading in a chilling grin. "Don't get any ideas about following us." The woman looked at Jordan, who was on one knee again as if she could pounce at the woman at any second. "Or you may live to regret it." She pressed the barrel of the gun further into Adley's temple.

Adley's shaky gaze met Jordan's, and her gaze softened. "It's going to be okay," she said, hoping she sounded more reassuring that she felt. Her hands were shaking, something that never happened unless Daisy was in danger. But this was different.

"I wouldn't be so sure about that." The woman sneered. Adley worked up the courage to meet Dresden's eye, and they exchanged a thousand words between a split second. The woman walked over to the other end of the warehouse, her gun still pressed against Adley's head, as one of the Agents dragged open the heavy metal door. The four Agents as well as their injured comrades piled into the van outside and drove away, Adley in hand.

CHAPTER SIX

The second that the Agents were out of their sight, Jordan leaped up, pushing herself up with her arms. She hissed in pain and covered her wound with her hand once again. She ran over to Daisy and put her non-bloody hand on her shoulder before cupping her chin with both hands.

"Are you okay?" Jordan asked frantically, inspecting Daisy for signs of further injury. Daisy coughed, and a few droplets of blood splattered onto Jordan's jacket, but Jordan ignored them. "I'm sorry, I should have protected you, I—"

"No," Dresden muttered, still on one knee, looking down at the ground.

"What?" Jordan looked up in surprise.

"You shouldn't have," he growled.

Jordan slowly stood, gently releasing Daisy's chin from her hands. "Excuse me?" She inclined her head toward him.

"You should have protected *HIM!*" Dresden shouted, shooting up and lunging at Jordan.

"Woah!" Jordan exclaimed as Dresden tackled her to the ground. He grabbed Jordan's wrists and attempted to pin her down. The sudden forced movement of her wounded arm caused her to scream in pain, and she kicked him in the chest in order to dislodge him.

Jordan rolled backward, jumping up to her feet. She watched as Dresden ran back toward her, his eyes burning with fury. He aimed a punch at her jaw, but she grabbed his wrist and twirled him around, pinning his arm between his shoulder blades with her uninjured arm.

"Connors, I'm not going to fight you," she grunted, holding the Agent firmly.

"Oh, you know all about not fighting back, don't you?" He snapped, his accent more pronounced than ever as he bent down suddenly, throwing Jordan over his head. She grunted as she landed hard on her back, her eyes squeezing shut. She remained on the floor for a moment, sent into a coughing fit as her body attempted to regain the breath that had been knocked out of her lungs as she covered her wound with her hand again.

Her eyes fluttered open again as she continued to cough, and she watched as Dresden stormed over to her. Her eyes widened, and she quickly stood as best she could, looking down to see blood now streaming down her arm, soaking into her jacket.

Jordan's tone grew concerned, but she tried to mask it. "Dresden, I know you're upset…" His first name felt awkward coming out of her mouth as she slowly backed away from him.

"Upset? I'm not upset," Dresden spoke in a sinister tone. Suddenly, a sharp kick to the chest shoved Jordan onto the ground again, causing her to let out a small squeak. "I'm *pissed.*" He walked toward Jordan, who scrambled backward despite the pain shooting through her.

"Just think about this…" Jordan's tone grew shakier, much to her chagrin.

Dresden packed a vicious right hook that came in contact with her jaw, the force of his anger making it a much more crippling blow. She let out a small whimper of pain. "He's gone! They took him!" Dresden yelled.

Jordan scrambled back farther, and her back hit the wall. She gulped. "D-Dresden…."

"It's all. Your. Fault!" He screamed, raising his foot to kick her. She flinched, shielding her face.

"I know!" Jordan yelled, wincing as her voice cracked.

"Connors!" Daisy shouted angrily, her voice shaking. She had stood up and now had her pistol trained on the Agent.

Dresden's foot froze in mid-air as Jordan awaited the impact that never came. She slowly opened her eyes and watched as Dresden lowered his foot. She cautiously sat up again as she shot Daisy a glance to tell her it was alright, and she holstered the pistol. She covered her wound again, trying to make the burning stop. "I should have protected him. I could have. I was right there. I could have touched him. I should have done something. I should have made them take me instead. I-I'm… sorry." Jordan shook her head, collapsing against the wall.

Dresden paused, taking a step toward Jordan. Jordan flinched, reflexively raising her hands in a fighting position, but she looked more nervous than intimidating. He felt a twinge of guilt. The redheaded Agent knelt down next to her, awkwardly placing his hand on her shoulder. He never was very good at comforting people.

"No, it's not. There's nothing you could have done. You were protecting him by cooperating. If you hadn't done what they wanted, they would have…" Dresden stopped, a lump forming in his throat.

"It's okay." Jordan met Dresden's eye. "He's going to be alright. He can take care of himself. Right now, we need to take care of you. We will find him, I promise. But you need to get some rest."

"Where am I supposed to go?" His British accent had faded away again, replaced by his American one. He shook his head. "I can't go back home. Not without Adley."

"I have a guest room… if you'd like to stay with me until we get Adley back…" Jordan muttered.

"You'd do that for me?" Dresden asked, surprised. "I just beat the crap out of you…"

"I deserved it," she muttered. "Plus, this way, I can keep an eye on you and make sure you don't do anything stupid." She nudged him playfully.

Dresden smiled, but it looked more forced than genuine. Jordan stood, extending the hand of her good arm to the tall Agent, who took it. She pulled him to his feet, not attempting to break all of the bones in his hand this time.

Daisy walked over and picked up her throwing knife, looking up as Jordan walked over.

"Are you alright?" Daisy's eyebrows were knitted with concern. She had never gotten shot; she didn't know how it felt.

"It's alright, just a flesh wound." Jordan winked at her, reminding her of Adley. The taller woman ran her fingers over the bullet hole in her jacket. "I'm going to have to put in a request to get my suit repaired, though." She sighed. "The Director isn't going to be happy."

"I'm sure the Director has loads of extra jackets laying around," Dresden muttered, attempting to force a smile.

"No, not that. This was our first contact with enemy Agents as a team, and one of our Agents got…" Jordan gulped. "I'll tell him. It was my fault, anyway; it's my responsibility."

"He's my partner," Dresden objected. "I should be the one to tell him."

Jordan shook her head. "No, I don't want him to take his anger out on you guys. It's my fault, I'll tell him. Come on, guys; we should get going."

●　　●　　●

"How could that possibly have happened?!" the Director exclaimed.

Jordan stood in front of the Director's desk, her hands clasped behind her back, her face entirely neutral despite the itchy bandage that was wrapped around her bicep. "It was my fault, sir. I should have been watching him."

The Director shook his head. "I don't understand. Agent Neilson was—still is—one of the highest-ranking Agents. There aren't many Gold Agents left—"

"Excuse me, sir?" Jordan interrupted. "Are you saying Agent Neilson is a Gold Level Agent?"

The man nodded. "Yes, Miss O'Connell, Agent Neilson is an Alpha-Nine. The youngest Agent ever to reach Gold Level. He was only a few years older than you." He watched as Jordan struggled to make her face remain neutral out of shock. "I will grant you the clearance for Agent Neilson's file. Usually, you have to be a Gold Level Agent in order to be given access, but this is a unique circumstance. However, this information is still classified at the highest level. The rest of your team is not permitted access to the file, understood?"

Jordan nodded. "Yes, sir. Thank you, sir. We will get Agent Neilson back, I'm sure of it."

"There is some information in that file that I believe you may find useful."

"Thank you, sir. I will inform the others." Jordan bowed her head to the Director before turning to exit the office.

•　　•　　•

Daisy was sitting on Dresden's desk as he paced around, nervously twirling his cane. Daisy suddenly shot up when Jordan entered the room.

"How did it go? What did he say?"

"I was right; he wasn't happy." Jordan looked at the floor. "But he did grant me access to Adley's file." She turned to Daisy. "Did you know he's a Gold Level?"

"What? No way!" Daisy bounced excitedly.

Jordan nodded. "Normally GLA files are classified for Gold Agents only, but the Director granted me access. The only problem is…" She trailed off.

"He only granted it to you, didn't he?" Dresden spoke for the first time since she had entered the small cubicle.

Jordan nodded sheepishly. "I'm sorry. But we're still on this mission together." She lifted Dresden's chin with her index finger, forcing him to meet her eye. "We're going to find him, I promise."

"I should update the mission log," Dresden muttered.

"Are you sure? I can do it if you like." It had only been a couple of hours, but Dresden looked drastically different. He had worry lines seemingly carved into his face around his eyes, and his posture was hunched over, leaning on his cane for support. It was as if he had aged years in just hours.

He shook his head. "No, I can do it. You should go take a look at that file."

Jordan hesitated before nodding her head. "Alright. Well, you know where my cubicle is if you need me."

"I'll try to see if I can track the van again." Daisy took out her laptop and took off the black cover. She opened it, but nothing happened. She pressed the power button. Nothing. "What? Why won't it…"

"I think I've located your problem." Jordan closed Daisy's laptop and flipped it over, revealing a bullet hole in the bottom.

Daisy's face went pale. "No…"

"What's the matter?" Dresden asked.

"She got that laptop when she reached Silver Level last month," Jordan explained.

"You can use my desktop if you wish. You should have authorization since we're working together," Dresden offered, his voice growing softer until the two of them barely heard the last word.

"Thanks," Daisy placed her broken laptop on the desk. "I'll let you do your mission log first."

Jordan nodded, strolling out of the room and into her own cubicle.

Jordan sat at her desk and turned on her desktop. The light flicked on, and a small computerized voice spoke.

"Vocal confirmation please."

"O'Connell, Jordan Marie," Jordan spoke, listening as the small chip in her desktop chirped with confirmation.

"Welcome, Agent O'Connell."

Jordan brought her cursor to the Agency files, bringing up all the records in the Agency's history. She hovered her cursor over the tabs on the left hand of the screen: *Current Missions, New Recruits, Overseas Missions, Mission Logs, Partner Assignments, there it is, Recently Granted.* She clicked on the tab, bringing up all the files she had been given access to during the last month. There it was, at the top of the screen, *Agent File; Agent Adley Neilson.* She clicked on the file and watched as the full file graced her screen for the first time. There was always something rather satisfying about seeing a file after the Director removed the black bars highlighting the classified bits. She began to read.

> **Agent:** *Adley Kepauch Neilson*
> **Codename:** *Rosie*
> **Age:** *30*
> **Date of Birth:** *April 17*
> **Agent Level:** *Alpha-Nine*
> **Mission Totals:** *151:9*
> **Partner History:** *Agent Bernstroff (previous); Agent Connors (previous)*
> **Kill Strikes:** *127:372*
> **Strengths:** *Disguise, Undercover*
> **Weapon of Choice:** *Sword*
> **Additional Information:** *Presently taken over as secretary*
> **Access Medical File**

She read over Adley's rather impressive record, noting his Mission Totals and Kill Strikes. According to the file, out of 160 total missions, only nine of them had either been unsuccessful or aborted and out of 372 chances he had to kill someone on a mission, he had only taken 127 lives. Not as high of a ratio as some other Agents, but also not the lowest. Some Agents, like Daisy, preferred not to kill and were very skilled in non-lethal incapacitation. Jordan didn't kill unnecessarily, but only if an innocent, or another Agent was threatened.

Jordan clicked on the attachment at the bottom of the page, attempting to open Adley's medical file, where she could access information that they collect in the Med Department, as well as records of any injuries he might have acquired during missions. Her lips twisted into a frown when the words *Access Denied* flashed across her screen.

Her mind wandered, dragging her off task. She went back to the menu and accessed Dresden's file. He was of lower rank than her, so she had access to his entire file already.

> **Agent:** *Dresden Scott Connors*
> **Age:** *26*
> **Date of Birth:** *December 21*
> **Agent Level:** *Alpha-Seven*
> **Mission Totals:** *127:4*
> **Partner History:** *Agent Haynes (previous); Agent Neilson (previous)*
> **Kill Strikes:** *151:167*
> **Strengths:** *Sniper*
> **Weapon of Choice:** *Sniper, Assault Rifle*

Additional Information:
Sniper Record: *123:0*
<u>**Access Medical File**</u>

That's one of the best sniper records I've ever seen. Jordan thought to herself. She thought about looking at his Medical File again, but she knew nothing would have changed; the only thing that wasn't classified was his past injuries record. She shook her head, telling herself to get back on track. *There has to be something here to help Adley.*

She went back to her Recently Granted files, but before she could click on Adley's file again, a new file appeared at the top of the screen entitled *Tech Design: Agent Watch.* It was classification level Platinum. Only Agents above Alpha-Ten were allowed to access it. Her heart skipped a beat. Were there any Platinum Agents left? She shook her head. Just one. The Director.

She selected the file, bringing up the schematics of the watch. Everyone in the Agency was given one when they reached Alpha-Zero. Before that, they were a level Beta. Nothing more than an intern, really. The watch embellishments were a symbol of your rank. Gold Level Agents had gold embellished watches; Silver Level Agents had silver, et cetera. If Adley's watch hadn't been hidden under the cuff of his suit jacket, she would have discovered his rank much sooner than she had.

She poured over the different abilities the watch had. Of course, there was the Mission Log Recorder and the Distress Signal, but there were features here that even *she* didn't know about. Suddenly, she froze in the middle of scrolling. She bolted out of her chair and ran to Dresden's cubicle.

•　　　•　　　•

Dresden sat in his desk chair for the first time in two days. The last time he sat here, he had been on the phone with the King of Qatar, messaging Adley. He sighed. He should never have dragged Adley into this.

He looked up at Daisy, who gave him a reassuring nod. He pressed the button on the side of his watch.

"Mission Log One Dash Six, Mission Code Name Masterpiece, February Fifth, Eleven Hundred hours, Agent Dresden Connors. There was a complication in the mission field. Adle—Agent Neilson was…" He searched for the right word. "Captured. Multiple armed assailants were guarding the warehouse, and they attacked the four of us. Agent O'Connell sustained an injury, but she paid a visit to the medical wing, and they patched it up. We are now focused on, ah, getting Agent Neilson back.

Safely." Dresden's voice cracked on the last word, a lump forming in his throat. "This, this is Agent, Agent D-Dresden Connors, signing off." He pressed the button on the side of his watch before crumbling down in his seat, burying his head in his arms on the desk.

Suddenly, Jordan ran into the room. "Guys!" She yelled, causing Dresden to jump, falling out of his chair in surprise.

"Bloody—what is it?" Dresden asked from where his chair had clumsily dumped him on the floor.

Jordan grinned. "I know how we can get Adley back."

CHAPTER SEVEN

Using her key, Jordan opened the door to her apartment, wincing slightly after pushing it open with her wounded arm. Dresden set his cane in the nearby umbrella stand, next to a black umbrella with a light-colored wooden handle that seemed strangely out of place in the clean and simply furnished apartment. The door opened up into a large multipurpose room dominated by a black leather couch and a sleek black table surrounded by chairs of the same color. The carpet seemed to be a dingy off-white, but he couldn't tell if it was supposed to be like that or if it was caused by a lack of vacuuming. The light fixtures were art deco, mostly metal, and the kitchen, although designed in a blockier style, still had a traditional feel to it. The furnishings were a tribute to Jordan's personality: functional, yet with a mind of their own, and a peculiar sense of home-away-from-home and a love for order and method.

"The guest room is in there; my room is right next door. If you need anything, don't hesitate to ask."

"It must be nice to have a guest room. Adley turned ours into a giant walk-in closet and painted very time-consuming and odd-looking flowers on all the walls." Dresden chuckled to himself, but it came out sounding forced.

Jordan turned to see that the tall Agent had suddenly become very interested in his shoes. "Hey," she said, her voice suddenly becoming gentle. "We're going to get him back, I promise."

Dresden met Jordan's gaze. His eyes looked even more like small Caribbean oceans now that they were swimming with tears.

She had taken off her letter jacket and turned it in earlier to get it repaired, and, minus the bandage she had wrapped around her right bicep, her arms were now exposed, something she wasn't used to. Dresden could tell, as she kept crossing and uncrossing her arms.

"Daisy should be here soon with your things; I'm having her drop them off."

Dresden wandered into the kitchen and peered into the pantry. Suddenly, he collapsed. Jordan cursed, rushing over to Dresden's side. "Dresden? Dresden are you alright?" She watched as Dresden's eyes fluttered open. "What happened?"

"Your pantry..." he whispered.

"What? What is it?"

"All you have is *Ramen Noodles*. What am I going to do with this cardboard in a bag? I didn't even eat this bad during my first week of Agency training."

Jordan slapped Dresden in the chest.

"Ow, what was that for?" Dresden chuckled.

"You scared me!"

The Tin Man laughed sincerely for the first time since Adley was taken. "Terribly sorry, I didn't mean to frighten you." He took Jordan's hand as she extended it, helping him to his feet.

Jordan playfully punched him in the arm, causing him to chuckle. "Hey, maybe you can make me some of those macaroons."

"Ah, well, um, baking is very... therapeutic... for me, so, ah, I wouldn't mind," Dresden stuttered.

"Therapeutic? How so?" she asked, opening her refrigerator in search of any sort of food, or anything that wasn't expired.

"Oh, ah, er, well, sometimes work gets a bit, ah, stressful for me so... I ah, make myself at home in the kitchen for a bit." He occupied his hands by buttoning and unbuttoning the cuff of his letter jacket.

"Training usually helps get my mind off of things," Jordan responded absentmindedly, sighing as she closed the fridge.

"Do you get stressed much?"

Jordan froze, surprised by the question.

"Ah, personal, sorry, stepping on toes again, not wanted," he quickly corrected himself.

Jordan opened her mouth to speak, but there was a knock on the door that interrupted her train of thought. Daisy came strolling into the kitchen with a black duffel bag. "Hello, I believe this is yours," she smiled at Dresden, handing him the bag.

"Thanks, Daisy." Jordan held up her fist, and the smaller Agent met it with her own.

"Don't thank me yet." Daisy smiled mischievously.

Dresden shot Jordan a questioning look, but she just smiled.

Daisy walked back out the front door, returning a few moments later with an armful of plastic grocery bags. "I'm not sure if you're aware," Daisy began, dumping the bags onto the kitchen counter, "but all this girl has in her pantry are Ramen Noodles and Mac and Cheese."

"Oh, I'm rather aware." Dresden arched an eyebrow at Jordan.

"I might have called in a few favors." Jordan grinned, taking out a can of pineapples from one of the bags. "What do you say you get your mind off of things for a while?"

"Well, I'm off to get back to work on tracking Adley down, just thought I'd stop by and say hey." Daisy looked over at Dresden. "I'm getting close."

"I told you, we're going to find him." Jordan smiled reassuringly.

"I'll let you know if I find anything. Toodles!" Daisy skipped out the door, closing it behind her.

•　　•　　•

Daisy walked into her apartment and sat down at her desktop, the familiar whirring noise as the computer started up making her smile. It quickly turned into a frown as she recalled the fate of her laptop and the capture of Agent Neilson. Determined, she opened her security feed and the tracking system to begin a full-scale infrared scan of the areas most likely to contain the blond Agent. While waiting for the scan to commence, she suddenly remembered Jordan telling her to update the mission log with any new information. Daisy pressed the button on her watch and began recording.

"Mission Log One Dash Seven, Mission Code Name Masterpiece, February Fifth, Twenty Hundred hours, Agent Daijeé Muhuaná. I've launched a full-area scan for Agent Neilson using the last known signal from the Agent Watch assigned to him, and I've narrowed the search down to roughly three pockets of land with a dense criminal population and similar signals according to the recent broadband from these three areas. With any luck, I will have his exact coordinates by tomorrow. This is Agent Daijeé Muhuaná, signing off."

•　　•　　•

"Toodles," Dresden mumbled. "Sounds like something he would say."

"Hey, I'm going to go put your bag in your room, I'll be right back. Maybe you can make some macaroons," Jordan teased, walking into the guest room. She was making the bed when she heard a sound that she immediately recognized as shattering glass. She rushed to the living room to find Dresden sat in the middle of what used to be a cerulean and white patterned vase, but was now merely shards of glass.

"Oh my—" Jordan rushed over to Dresden, ignoring the little fragments of glass getting stuck in the bottoms of her feet. She grabbed Dresden by the arm and carefully led him, with much resistance, away from the broken glass. "Are you alright? What happened?"

Dresden had his eyes squeezed shut, which buried them in the wrinkles of his forehead and the corner of his eyes. When the redhead spoke, his voice was hoarse, and his British accent was present in every word.

"It's unbelievable but undeniable; I ruin everything. I'd better go home; I'm infringing on your hospitality enough, I don't want you to get tangled up in this mess." Jordan sat him on the couch and had to fight him to roll up his sleeve to examine a cut with a large chunk of the vase in it. She rushed out of the room. He continued to talk, but now it was just to himself.

"Lives are like butterfly wings: You touch them, they die. It's much better to observe the beauty from afar. When you interfere, Connors, it ends in brokenness. You'll never be good enough, smart enough, special enough, to rise up. Nothing in your future, just another cog in the murder machine, the murderer of well-planned dreams."

Jordan came back with a medicine chest and worry on her face. "Dresden?" She shook the Agent vigorously, and he attempted to squirm away. The concern in her face turned quickly to anger. "Dresden, snap out of it." She pushed his chin up to force him to meet her gaze, although his eyes were still forcefully closed. "Talk to me," she pleaded, her voice softening again.

"I just wanted to admire it a bit; it looked like something Adley would paint. But now it's gone. Now they're both gone." Additional tears formed in the man's vivid blue-green eyes, only causing them to become more vibrant.

"Hey, listen, it's alright. It's just a vase. And Adley's not gone, he's not going to give up. He needs you not to give up either. Here, let me see your arm." She pulled out a bottle of hydrogen peroxide and some gauze from the box of miscellaneous medical supplies. Dresden hesitantly stuck out his arm, allowing Jordan to roll up his sleeve again, revealing the deep cut on his forearm, a shard of the glossy blue glass still lodged in his arm. "How did you manage to drop the vase, and then somehow get a shard of it in your arm?" What ordinarily would have been a humorous statement became a genuine question as Jordan's tone became concerned.

"I was trying to pick up the glass, and I slipped. My arm slammed onto the floor, and a piece of glass got stuck," Dresden muttered.

He winced slightly as she touched the glass. "This might hurt a little," Jordan warned.

"It's alright, I can handle—" Dresden was cut off by Jordan quickly dislodging the shard from his arm, and swore under his breath.

"I'm sorry, are you alright?" Jordan sounded concerned as she inspected his cut for any further shards.

The tall Agent only nodded, not trusting the words that could come out if he opened his mouth.

"I'm going to clean the wound now, okay?" Jordan asked, reaching for the bottle of hydrogen peroxide and a small dishcloth. She wet it with the antiseptic, gently pressing it against the cut.

Dresden flinched, attempting to pull his arm away from Jordan, but she tightened her grip around his wrist, not allowing him to move his arm. "I would think that someone who's been shot before would be alright with a little hydrogen peroxide…" she teased, recalling his file as she reached for the gauze.

"I suppose this must be an entirely different light you're seeing me in now," Dresden mumbled, attempting to pull himself together.

"I never would have suspected that the tin man had a heart after all." Jordan looked up at him to see his reaction to her teasing.

"We're not supposed to. We were taught since day one not to let our emotions get in the way of the mission, both of us. Emotions are a distraction; they get in the way. That's why the Agency implemented that blasted policy about romantic relationships between partners," he muttered, watching as Jordan unraveled the roll of gauze, slowly removing the now blood-soaked washcloth from his arm.

"I remember those lessons." She nodded, beginning to wrap his arm in the gauze. She paused a moment before looking up into his eyes, still sparkling with unshed tears. She sighed. "I usually don't get… emotionally attached to people. Cliché, I know, but it works. If you don't care about anyone, those emotions can't cloud your judgment. They can't distract you. I've been on a couple of dual-pair missions before. It was only about the mission. There were no dinners, no sparring together, only working. No emotional attachment. It was easier that way. I got too attached to my first partner, before Daisy. Agent Rachel Sturges. I learned the hard way how that ends. She…" Jordan tried to find the right words, but she simply couldn't. "She fell… on a mission. Taking a bullet for me, no less." She cleared her throat, trying to focus on bandaging Dresden's arm. "I promised myself I wouldn't get emotionally attached again. I went solo for a couple of months, but the Director called me in one day and said he had a new Agent who had just joined and needed a partner, Daisy. I couldn't say no to the Director, so I reluctantly accepted." She shook her head. "I don't know why I'm telling you this."

"No, you can keep going. I mean, ah, if you want to. It's good to hear that I'm not the only one here with a tragic backstory." Another forced chuckle escaped Dresden's lips.

Jordan stopped wrapping the gauze for a moment, looking up at Dresden, unsure if he were joking or not. "Are you actually interested, or are you just being polite?"

"No, I really am." He nodded, his red hair flying about his head.

Jordan paused for another moment before releasing a deep sigh and continuing with the gauze. "Well, I found myself slowly getting attached to Daisy. At first, I tried to fight it, but that didn't work. So instead, I decided that I would protect her. So I have. I've done everything I can to protect her. I'd do anything to protect her." She finally finished wrapping the gauze as she finished talking.

Dresden nodded, and at that moment, Jordan realized that he felt the same about his own partner.

"I'm sorry, I didn't mean—"

"It's alright," Dresden quickly cut her off.

Jordan's face fell. She hesitantly met Dresden's eye again. "What about you? Do you form emotional attachments easily?"

Dresden froze, and now it was Jordan's turn to look at her shoes. "Sorry, I shouldn't have asked. I'm too nosy." She got up and started walking toward the kitchen again to put the bloody washcloth in the sink. He opened his mouth to speak, but instead, his eye caught on a prescription pill bottle poking out of the box of miscellaneous medical supplies.

"What's this?" he asked, tilting his head slightly, reaching out with his good arm and plucking the small bottle from the box.

Jordan looked up from the floor as she walked back from the kitchen, her eyes widening as she saw Dresden reach for the bottle. "It's nothing," she said quickly as she ran toward him, snatching the bottle from his hand. She winced at the movement, putting her hand over her wound again as Dresden looked at her in surprise.

"S-sorry, I don't know how that got in there," Jordan stuttered, going into the kitchen and placing the pills in the cabinet. She walked back to the living area and put the hydrogen peroxide and the gauze back in the box before picking it up and taking it back to the bathroom.

Dresden heard some muffled swearing, followed by a barrage of insults, come from behind the door that Jordan had shut on her way into the bathroom. He sat there on the couch for a minute, staring at the broken glass scattered about the floor.

He sighed. The Agent thought for a moment, and finally, after glancing up to check if Jordan was coming, walked over to the kitchen and opened the cabinet where Jordan had hidden the container. He grabbed the pill bottle and rotated it until he found the label. He read the name. *Fluoxetine.*

"Dresden?" Jordan's voice sounded small and innocent behind him, which was somehow scarier than if she would have yelled. Dresden jumped, quickly spinning around, the bottle still in his hand. Jordan's eyes fell on the cylindrical container, but rather than becoming mad as he had expected, there was something hidden behind her eyes that he had never imagined seeing.

Fear.

"W-what are these?" Dresden asked nervously.

Jordan suddenly looked defeated. "I-I—" She stuttered, but stopped, not knowing what to say.

"Jordan." Dresden looked at her, using her first name for the first time. She finally met his eye. "You can tell me."

Jordan sighed. "Come here." She grabbed the wrist of Dresden's non-injured arm and led him over to the living area, carefully walking around the shattered glass that she seemed to have no intention of cleaning up. She sat him on the couch, and plopped down next to him, facing him, but not meeting his eye.

"Jordan, what is it? What's the matter?" Dresden asked, his British accent returning.

Jordan suddenly brought her knees up close to her chest, wrapping her arms around them and burying her head.

"Jordan? Jordan, what's wrong?" This was the first time that he had seen the seemingly fearless Agent like this, and it was startling, to say the least. She said nothing. Instead, she only sat there. Dresden hesitated before putting his hand on her shoulder. "Jordan?" His voice dropped to a soft whisper.

Jordan moved her mouth away from her knees just enough to give her room to speak. "Do you really want to know what the medication is for?"

"Yes, I do." Dresden shifted his hand on Jordan's shoulder, trying to make her face him.

Jordan sighed, slowly lifting her head. "You can't tell anyone, alright? Promise me you won't tell anyone."

Dresden put his hand under her chin, making her look at him. "I promise."

Jordan gently took the bottle from Dresden's hand and held it up to his eye level, which, since he was slouching to meet her eye, was at the same level as hers. "It's an antidepressant," she muttered, running her finger along the label.

Dresden's eyes widened with surprise. "Oh." The bigger Agent didn't seem to know what to say. Jordan didn't blame him, though. "If you, ah, don't mind me asking, ah, how long have you…" he trailed off, unable to finish his sentence.

"Since middle school. But I wasn't officially diagnosed until my first year of high school." She shook her head. "I was bullied a lot. Everything I did was an invitation for everyone to make fun of me. That's how I learned to fight so well—years of defending myself. I had skipped two grades in elementary school, thanks to my eidetic memory, so I was the youngest by at least that many years. I was smaller than a lot of the kids in my grade as well, despite being tall for my age. I got written up for fighting a lot, even though I had only been acting in self-defense. So, I was the 'smart' kid to the teachers, but the troublemaker to the administrators. Then, toward the end of high school, when I was fifteen, I was approached by someone from the Agency. They said they had a position open, and 'could use someone of my skill set,' and that's how I ended up here."

The two of them sat in silence for a moment, neither exactly sure of what to say. Jordan finally broke the silence again. "I understand if you want to reassign, Daisy can track down Adley; you really don't need my help. I'm sorry that I dragged you into all of this." Dresden saw that brown eyes were now glazed with tears.

"Hey." He placed his hand on Jordan's knee, and Jordan slowly uncurled herself. "I never said I was going anywhere. You had my back, and now I have yours. This doesn't change anything. Why should it?"

Jordan met Dresden's eye, blinking back her tears. "Thank you." She barely managed to choke out the words before clearing her throat. "What about you? You've heard my depressing backstory, what's yours?" She chuckled, attempting to lighten the mood.

"I think I might actually have you beat on this one." Dresden's eyes twinkled with a mischievous glint.

Jordan arched an eyebrow. "Is that so? Okay then, go ahead, tell me."

Dresden cleared his throat, crossing his legs at the knees. "Ready for a heart-wrenching blockbuster?"

The corners of Jordan's mouth twisted into a barely suppressed smile. "Go ahead, Seven."

In a fully exaggerated British accent, Dresden launched into a similar tale. "When I was only a small disappointment, and my grandfather was only a slight alcoholic, I was consistently lonely and had approximately one friend, so I turned to the voices in my head instead of the ones around me. Unfortunately, the voices in my head were not the friendly type. They were more of the 'you're a worthless child and will die all alone with only your self-hate and a dead cat in a well,' kind of voices. Of course, I can't do anything right, and sooner or later, their predictions came true—a self-fulfilling prophecy.

"Of course, it wasn't truly my fault; children absorb the environment around them. My grandfather wasn't truly a bad person; he just had misplaced anger and two live punching bags on which to take it out, my sister and I. When he died right before my third year of high school, he only left me one thing in this world: a box of hate mail about how much I was 'a bastard through and through,' 'no kin of his', and 'the kid who stares with those psycho eyes,' who would 'amount to as much as your whore mother.' So, not self-induced at all.

"I made a plan right before my first year of high school: I would join the Marines for active duty, my sister would be a forensic pathologist at her early college, and we would both get drafted away from Grandfather. In school, I tried to prove him wrong by striving to be the best, but I spiraled out of control very quickly, as I developed quite the anxiety problem. The only person I could talk to was my sister. It wasn't as if I could talk to Grandfather about it, so I never got any actual help. My biggest problem wasn't that I was afraid of people: I can't talk to individuals whom I believe hate me, and of course, no one wanted to talk to such a pitiful yet intimidating child. Practically every kid was afraid of me, the 'redhead stalker,' and I once again became an outcast. The only place I was truly accepted was in my ROTC group, where my nickname was 'Cyborg' because of my perfect combat strategies and my ability to distance from people, which of course was anxiety-based. These skills were brought to the Agency's attention in my third year, and they offered me early enrollment. Originally, I declined the invitation permanently. I had been accepted into West Point with an offer to begin active duty within the first semester, and the training I would receive there would put me at the top of the heap for practically any other position. About halfway through my training, the Director extended the invitation again due to short staffing. This time, however, my sister convinced me that the Agency held more potential than the field work and wouldn't be a desk job of espionage.

"Reluctantly, I agreed, and stalled the invitation until I finished my training at West Point, and then accepted.

"And that's how I met the precious flower child that is now my future husband, whenever I get around to marrying him," he finished nonchalantly.

"Oh." Jordan paused, entirely unsure of what to say. "Yeah, I think you have me beat there."

Dresden chuckled slightly, looking at his hands clasped in his lap. "I suppose we all have our issues."

"I suppose we do." Jordan nodded awkwardly, scuffing the toe of her boot around in the carpet.

"At least having anxiety makes you a better strategist…" Dresden trailed off, attempting to put a more optimistic spin on the situation.

"Or threat assessment Agent," Jordan muttered under her breath, and Dresden looked up at her.

"You too?" he asked, surprised.

"Not as bad, but, yeah. It sort of goes with the other thing, I guess," she muttered. "You've told Adley all of this?" she attempted to change the subject.

"Of course. We tell each other everything." Dresden sounded surprised at the question. He swallowed a lump that had gathered in his throat. "We *told* each other everything."

"Who else knows?" Jordan asked curiously.

"No one. Just you now, I suppose. These things are always classified in the Agent Files." Jordan nodded slightly, thinking back to the black bars covering up her problems. "I assume Daisy knows of yours as well?"

Jordan nodded.

"Anyone else?" Dresden asked.

Jordan shook her head. "No one to tell."

They sat in silence for some time, just sharing in each other's misery. Dresden's eyes darted toward the pieces of the vase on the floor, but it was a while before he voiced his thoughts. "I'll, ah, pick that up. Terribly sorry for all of this mess."

Jordan got up slowly, still studying her shoes. "Don't worry about it; I'll get it in a minute. You are a guest, after all."

She trudged back to where the beautiful cerulean pieces of glass were scattered across the carpet and began to scoop up the broken vase carefully.

Dresden watched her quietly, then got off the couch and softly walked up behind the blonde, making sure that she could see him coming; they didn't need another person to slice themselves open with glass, after all. He waited until she finished and put a reassuring hand on her shoulder. "I'm sorry for all of this I've ruined: the mission, your vase, your trust, our chances of getting back the painting. I ruin everything. You've been very kind and understanding, but I'll reassign. I wouldn't want to ruin your perfect mission success rate, after all." He blinked rapidly, struggling to keep in tears, the rawness of his voice only making his accent more beautiful. "I don't want you or Daisy to get hurt, either."

Jordan turned to face him, her voice soothing, like she was talking to a frightened animal. "The mission hasn't failed. We can still recover the painting, but our first priority is getting Adley back safely. It's not your fault. Not even I expected an ambush like this, and I'm a threat assessment operative. We were all taken off guard. Besides, we need you, remember? The Director said, 'This mission will require special skills that you all possess'," she quoted, lightly placing a hand on the redhead's uninjured arm. "What would happen without you?"

Suddenly, the taller Agent unburied his face from his hands and threw his arms around Jordan, pulling her into a tight hug as he finally started to cry. She was startled at first, as she wasn't exactly used to much affection toward her. Nevertheless, she hugged him back tightly. The floodgates broke, and Jordan felt Dresden's silent tears slide into her hair like rain as he held her close, an anchor in his remorse. Pressed against him, Jordan could feel the beating of the Tin Man's anguished, long-denied heart.

Between sobs, Dresden managed a few words. "I just hope Adley's alright."

CHAPTER EIGHT

Before Adley even opened his eyes, he knew he was tied to a chair. He could feel the prickling rope digging into his wrists behind his back, which meant something even worse. Those blasted Agents had taken his jacket. Adley's favorite pocket square was in that jacket.

Only after he was certain no one else was in the room did he allow his eyes to flutter open, his vision blurred from being unconscious for so long—blasted chloroform.

As his vision was returning, he saw an unmistakably familiar pattern.

"Ah, hallo Miss Trombone, how are you today?" he muttered, still slightly delirious from the chemicals used to sedate him. However, when his vision cleared, it revealed that it wasn't her after all, just an old couch.

He took in every detail of his surroundings, trying to determine where he was. His chair was in the middle of a dingy room, the walls were off-white, or perhaps they used to be white judging by the splotches of the dirt. The couch directly in front of him had a black and white floral cover that *definitely* looked like something Miss Tyrannosaurus would wear. There was a small rectangular wooden table sitting in front of the sofa, with a small lamp that was a singularly nasty shade of green, one of the very few light sources in the room. The carpet was an utterly *horrid* shade of, was that *navy blue*? Adley had to fight to keep down his breakfast. There was only one wall furnishing in the entire room, a simple painting hanging above the couch. The painting depicted an ordinary field of flowers, something that Adley himself could have created, except in a much higher quality.

"Terrible brushstrokes, you can see them even from here. I'm no Leonardo Da-Vinci, but I can paint better than that! *Terrible* color coordination, everyone knows that blue and orange don't mix well, especially in oils. What I wouldn't give to redecorate this room!" Adley sighed, clearly more exasperated by the decorations than his capture.

Out of habit, his finger found the mission log recorder button on his watch, and he instantly began to update it. "Mission Log One Dash… Eight I'm assuming, Mission Code Name Masterpiece, February Fifth, unsure of the time, Agent Adley Neilson. I have been captured and am currently being held in what looks to be the basement of a very outdated building, judging by the decor. Honestly, this stuff seems like it came straight out of Miss Train Track's wardrobe. Anyhoo, the point is, so far I haven't seen or heard anything of importance to the mission, but I'll try to keep you lovely people posted. This is Agent—"

The door slowly swung open, and the woman who had captured him sauntered into the room, her cream heels sinking into the terrible carpet. As she straightened up, Adley got a close look at her for the first time.

She was small and lithe, and couldn't be much shorter than him. Judging by her features, which were amplified by approximately half a palette of blue eyeshadow and blood-red matte lipstick, she wasn't any older than twenty, although she carried herself like a much older woman. Her black hair was in a braid which she tossed over her shoulder, and her dark brown skin caused her muddy eyes to glow with an odd light. She was wearing a cream business suit with a flared skirt and form-fitted blazer, and he could just see a small part of a navy blue striped shirt peeking out of the jacket. When she realized that he was watching her, the woman shot him a knowing smirk and produced from her breast pocket a very familiar looking navy pocket square.

Adley shot her a nasty look. "That one's my favorite, give it back," he said, using a colder tone than he had ever since he stepped down from Gold.

The woman ambled over to him, dangling the fabric between two fingers just out of his reach if he hadn't been restrained. "I don't think so, Blondie. We have not yet been properly introduced, so I can't do you *any* favors. My name is of no importance, but if you want, you can call me Drina." She smiled at the Agent, but it lacked the warmth of a natural smile, sending chills up Adley's spine. He didn't let it show, of course, and lifted his chin.

"Neilson, code 407," he said plainly, hearkening back to many encounters like this in his active-duty years. He felt a buzz at his wrist, notifying him that the watch was now on and ready to incognito record. Such function came in handy apprehending victims and kept the cases out of the public eye, where there were many horrendous-colored courtrooms and colorblind lawyers.

Drina, as she claimed to be called, clapped slowly. "A willing captive! It seems we picked the right one."

Adley raised an eyebrow. "I'm sure I don't know what you mean."

The woman smirked. "The boss said that the Agency would be alerted about the theft, and hopefully, there'd be enough Agents for one to be ripe for capture. You seemed to be the easiest to pick up."

Adley rolled his eyes, something that Dresden normally did, not the good-natured secretary. "Can we go ahead with the interrogations, so I have time to fit in lunch? I'm starving already."

Drina suddenly darted forward and packed a good punch to his stomach, causing a startled *oof* from the Agent. "With all that padding, I think we'll have to starve you for any of my torture methods to work," she commented snidely as she walked over to the opposite wall, pulling on the edge of the painting. It came out of the wall with a hydraulic squeak, using the couch as a step to get into the exposed hole behind the artwork. The thin woman stepped through the hole, calling over her shoulder to her captive. "Don't be sad about our brief interview; I'll be back soon with a couple of old friends." She swung her leg through the hole and vanished, pulling the painting back over the hole with a muffled clunk.

Adley shifted uncomfortably in his chair, gazing around the room once more and inconspicuously starting the recording. Torture and interrogation were no fun, but it was a fact of life as a Secret Agent. It came with the turf. He almost wished that couch *was* Miss Tangerine, that there was someone here who could feel emotion, someone he could talk to.

There was a creaking noise, and the painting swung out of the wall, admitting Drina back into the room. In her left hand, she was balancing a laptop with a handgun laying on top of it, and around her neck hung a pair of brass knuckles on a rather dingy chain.

She set the laptop on the table with the ugly lamp, typing furiously for a moment before turning away from the device in satisfaction. The handgun went into her blazer pocket, and she slipped on the brass knuckles, strolling closer to Adley. "Now, we're ready to begin," she said sweetly, with a false calm that made him want to punch her even more.

The woman began circling his chair even more insistently, resembling a cobra about to strike with the twitching movements of her body. "Let's start with some easy questions," she murmured, running her fingers across the metal on her hands once more, her copper-brown eyes meeting her prisoner's.

He met her gaze with a smirk. "Go ahead, *kõhnmadu.*"

She cleared her throat, one hand going automatically to her gun. "What are the names of the other two Agents who were with you and Jordan in the warehouse?"

Adley was startled by the mention of Jordan's name. "There was no one by that name present," he bluffed, hoping that the inquisitor wouldn't catch how nervous he was about this scrap of correct information.

Drina grinned unpleasantly. "My nickname in our organization is Bats: I hear everything from the drop of a hat to a Chinese girl screaming amid combat. Don't tell me my ears are lying to me."

Adley suddenly remembered the scene at the warehouse. Jordan getting shot. Daisy screaming her name. Dresden…

The plump Agent shook the thought away, playing it off as feigned surprise. "They call you Bats? I'm not sure that's accurate; to me, you're more like Guano," he snarked off playfully. The thinner Agent struck him a glancing blow on the cheek which wouldn't have hurt much without the added zing from the brass knuckles.

As Adley pretended to nurse his wound, the criminal Agent got very close to his face, her breath reeking of unbrushed teeth and eggs. "Listen, being smart won't help you at all in this situation. Cooperate, and maybe the CFH will leave your little friends alone," she said menacingly.

The blond *tsked* in annoyance. "Dah-ling, you're as fake as your eyelashes. You have as little power over the other Agents as I do over Miss Tapestry's terrible wardrobe. Can you believe she actually wore that same couch cover once? *Terrible* aesthetics. Why, the last time I saw her, she was dressed in a pink and lime green lace halter with—" The butt of the gun abruptly came down on his head, causing him to see stars swirling around Drina as she strolled out from behind him.

"I'm the one supposed to be asking the questions, you fat git," she drawled. "If I wanted you to go on about my decor, I would have hired an interior designer to come assess it."

Adley made a noise of disgust. "First, you insult me; then you undermine my decorative expertise? You're a terrible person, my lady. Respect your elders." The crook responded by giving him a backhand slap across his face, the cheap metal in the knuckles scraping against his skin. He made a small mewl of pain and kicked at his assailant. She wisely stepped out of kicking distance and stooped to grab something from under the hideous couch. She straightened up, holding a wicked-looking knife, a cold gleam in her eyes. "Right, now let's get down to business."

For about the thousandth time, Adley fervently wished that the Tech Department had re-installed his virtually undetectable blade into his watch so that he could slice up Guano like Dresden cut cake. Unfortunately, he was only an Agent again for this mission, so he didn't get his sword back. It was probably out of style by now, anyway.

Drina stalked back over to the center of the room where Adley was tied to the chair and stood behind him, shoving her arm with the knife in front of his face. "We're going to play Twenty Questions, alright? Do you know how to play the game?" she asked mockingly.

Adley pretended to think for a moment as his assailant untied his wrists from behind the chair and retied them to the arms of the chair. "Is this the game where I insult your furniture, and you give me a cookie afterward for winning?"

The knife swung closer to his throat, missing his goatee by a millimeter, and the woman snaked her head around his shoulder, hate burning in her eyes. "No, it's the game where you get a tally mark for every question you get wrong and win with the least points," she stated, her face twisting into a demented smile. "I forgot my notepad and pen upstairs, so we're going to keep track a different way."

Drina gradually lowered the knife down to his arm and rolled up the sleeve of his shirt. "Here's a point for me to start for all the insults you've thrown," she hummed with pleasure, making a deep cut about an inch long in the Agent's arm. He hissed in pain, the blood flowing from the deep cut staining the sleeve of his white shirt a soft crimson.

"You're ruining my only nice white shirt," he growled through gritted teeth.

"That's alright, you strike me as the sort of man who'd wear pink, anyway," the dark-skinned woman purred placidly, wiping the blood on the knife farther up on his sleeve. "Now that you know the rules, let's play."

She produced from the inner pocket of her blazer a wrinkled sheet of paper. Shaking it out, she began to recite the questions printed on it to her captive.

"How high up are you in the Agency?"

Flipping his hair as best he could with his hands tied and his arm freely bleeding, Adley attempted to mimic Dresden's accent. "Well, if you really must know, I just got promoted to head janitor last week."

Drina returned the knife to the blond's arm, making an identical cut next to the first. "That's one, you useless poof. It'll be a lot less painful for you if you just co-operate." She glanced at her laptop before asking the next question. "Who are your partners?"

"Your *motha.*"

Two. "Where did you get the coordinates for the warehouse?"

"Where you got your furniture: They're both terrible and out of date."

Three. "What is your full mission?"

"To sell you some new carpet, and that's some godawful upholstery."

Four. "Where is your employer located?"

"Where your fashion sense is, so you'd better start looking."

Drina dug the knife into his arm, causing a much deeper cut that caused him to yelp in pain.

"You're impossible," she said through gritted teeth.

"And so's your ignorance of makeup use. Eyeshadow palettes are supposed to be multiple-use, but evidently, you didn't get that memo. Honestly, with the super hearing and the horrendous makeup, you should join the circus. They always need more clowns."

The brown eyes of his interrogator glowed with the inner fire of fury. "You think you're hilarious, don't you, old man?" she sneered.

Adley shrugged. "They always say, be your own biggest fan."

Drina hit him in the gut with the handle of the blade. "You wouldn't be such a smart-ass if you knew what it's costing you," she growled.

Adley cocked an eyebrow. "Fill me in, drama queen."

She slapped him across the face with the broad-bladed knife. "While you were acting like a damsel in distress, one of my men shot a bullet with a tracker into the laptop of one of your little friends. We're tracking them as we speak."

Adley raised his head, but his voice shook a little. "You're a bigger liar than someone with plastic surgery."

She grinned evilly. "We'll see, tramp. Back to the game."

•   •   •

About an hour later, Drina removed the knife from the most recent incision and wiped it on Adley's bloodstained sleeve, the red and raw wounds forming twenty precise tally marks, plus one for good measure, testimonies of the failure of her inquisition. The Agent seemed unfazed by the pain of his injuries, although he had let out a hoarse scream during the last set of incisions.

The African-American woman carefully wrapped her knife up in the crumpled and sweaty sheet she had read her questions off of and tucked the blade into an inner pocket of her blazer. She cast a sharp glance at her prisoner, who had composed himself and was now looking at her with an air of expectancy.

"What? Care for another round?" she snapped, tired of the patronizing look on the Agent's face.

He shrugged. "Well, I just remembered a crucial element of the game rules. Traditionally, the other person playing the game gets to have a turn. I don't have my sword with me, unfortunately, or a pen, so may I borrow your knife?"

The thin criminal delivered a vicious punch to his face, darkening his left eye. "Shut up, you pixie-man," she snarled, drawing back her fist for another punch.

Adley smirked. "No, I don't think so. Pixie-man? My, you're running low on insults."

"You're very stubborn. I hope you cooperate better tomorrow," she said coldly, collecting her things and leaving the prisoner once more.

As soon as she left, Adley pressed the button on his watch, stopping the recording. He leaned back in his chair, staring at the horrendous painting on the wall as his mind wandered. He tried not to dwell on the pain in his arm as his mind grasped vainly at a scrap of conversation that he had with Guano. What was it? *Something essential, something about Daisy…*

He frowned, trying to recall what it was when suddenly it hit him like an ugly neon dress hits the red carpet.

The bullet.

His finger flew to his watch, and he began a Morse Code sequence.

Dot dotdot. Dash dashdash. Dot dotdot.

Hopefully, Drina had been bluffing.

CHAPTER NINE

Dresden was lying in bed in Jordan's guest room, trying to convince himself that Adley was alright. The vibration in his watch caused him to sit up with a start.

He immediately recognized the Morse Code. It was an S.O.S. signal.

He felt a surge of hope rise in his chest. When they had been a partner duo in the field, their watches had been synced with a feature that allowed them to send messages back and forth with the Agency's own code, which was much faster to type than morse code, in his opinion. The watch had never been reassigned, and for once, the redhead Agent was glad that half the Tech Department were total slackers.

There were so many things that Dresden wanted to say to Adley, so many words that he would want to have been the last he had said to his partner before he was captured, but he knew that he didn't have time. He instead tapped his watch strap once, the indication that he was listening, and pulled his phone out of his pocket to write what Adley dictated.

Tracker bullet. Daisy's laptop.

Dresden blinked in surprise, his finger hovering over the keys. He checked the time to see if it would be acceptable to shoot off a quick text to Daisy. When he discerned that it wasn't, he instead leaped out of bed, running into Jordan's room as three more words came through the watch.

I love you.

Dresden paused before bursting into Jordan's room.

Jordan lay asleep, sprawled out across her entire mattress. Her breathing was slow yet peaceful, and she was making little almost-snoring noises that sounded like a kitten wheezing. Dresden knew that she would not be happy being woken up, but this was urgent.

Suddenly, Jordan abruptly began to thrash in her sleep, whimpering like a wounded puppy. Dresden gently placed his hand on Jordan's shoulder, and he remembered when he had wrapped his arms around her only a few hours earlier. He quickly blushed but shook it off.

"Ah, Jordan?"

Jordan stirred, her eyes slowly fluttering open. Jumping when she saw the figure standing in front of her, her hand instantly went for the knife hidden under her headboard and held it out in front of her. "Hey, it's just me." Dresden's voice was gentle, attempting to calm Jordan.

She opened her eyes fully, allowing her vision to clear. "S-sorry," Jordan stuttered, putting the knife back in its hiding place. She looked back up at Dresden and jumped again.

"What? What is it?" Dresden asked, looking behind him.

Jordan chuckled a bit. "Your hair."

He hastily licked his palm and ran it over the frizzy red mass. "Ah, Adley's the one with the natural look. Mine requires some taming."

Jordan chuckled again. "So, what is it?"

"I just received word from Adley."

Jordan froze, the amused smile wiped from her face. "How?"

"The watch's code feature; Adley and I still have our watches synced."

"What did he say? Is he alright?"

"He couldn't say much, but remember the bullet that got lodged in Daisy's laptop?" Any semblance of Dresden's British accent was gone now, replaced by his American one.

"What about it?" Jordan's voice was raw with concern.

"It's a tracker."

Jordan was fully awake now. She jumped out of bed, still in her pajamas, which were really just a long sleeve shirt and a pair of sweatpants. She grabbed her phone from the nightstand and dialed Daisy's number. The phone rang three times before Daisy picked up.

"Jordan? It's three in the morning, what's wrong?" Dresden heard Daisy's voice from the other end, breathing a sigh of relief. He hadn't quite grown as attached to Daisy as he had to Jordan, but he would still hate for something to happen to her. He shot Jordan a quick look, wondering if she often called Daisy this late with something wrong.

"Daisy, we just heard from Adley. Yeah, the code feature. He's alright, as far as we can tell. Listen, you know the bullet that got stuck in your laptop? Adley said that it's a tracker. Please tell me you left your laptop at the Agency." Jordan instantly cursed herself at the thought. If she had left it, the whole Agency could be at risk, especially if they had more technology like this.

Her eyes widened, and for a split second Dresden swore he saw fear behind her eyes. "Daisy, get over here now, they could be tracking it."

Jordan heard a click at the other end. She looked up at Dresden. "She brought the laptop home."

Dresden swore. "Do you think they can get there that fast?"

"I don't know, but I don't want to find out." Jordan's voice cracked out of concern, and she began to pace back and forth in the small bedroom.

Jordan was still pacing ten minutes later when there was a knock on the door. Jordan leaped for the door, her hand on her pistol. She had put her holster back on, the only time she wasn't wearing it was if she was sleeping. Dresden had his sidearm as well, covering Jordan as he stood behind her, aiming at the door. Jordan looked through the peephole, looking over her shoulder and nodding at Dresden. She turned the handle. Dresden rested his finger on the trigger, his foot tapping.

"Easy, it's me." Daisy walked into the apartment, a duffel bag in hand.

They both sighed in relief, lowering their weapons. "Were you followed?" Jordan asked, closing the door and turning the lock.

"No, I wasn't. And I disabled any cameras that might pick me up as I left. These guys aren't messing around; I don't want to take any chances."

Dresden nodded, wanting to ask as to how she had managed this, but he kept quiet.

"We need to extract that bullet and disable it." Jordan had started pacing again.

"Where is it?" Dresden asked.

"Well, I have a bag with a lead lining, it's made to disable any GPS tracking."

"What bag?" Dresden stopped tapping his foot for a moment.

Daisy glanced down to the duffel bag in her hand.

"No way," Dresden muttered. "You brought that here?! Are you stupid?!" Dresden ran his fingers through his hair, an anxiety mannerism with which Jordan was rather familiar.

Daisy's face twisted into a frown.

"Hey, Daisy, can you take that to the study?" Jordan asked her partner, who nodded, walking through the living room and into a smaller room on the back wall, closing the door.

Jordan watched as Daisy left the room before turning back to Dresden and putting her hand on his shoulder. "Hey, it's okay, breathe, it's going to be fine," Jordan cooed as she soothed the anxious Agent.

"What if that bag doesn't work? What if they track that laptop? What if they got information out of Adley and they know who we are?" Dresden stuck his hands in his messy hair, which shook Jordan's hand off of his shoulder as he again tapped his foot nervously.

"Dresden, Dresden, listen to me. It's okay, I promise, it's going to be okay. Do you want to sit down?"

The tall Agent nodded, and Jordan led him to the couch, sitting next to him. She noticed that his foot had stopped tapping, hopefully a sign that he was calming down. "I've tested that bag myself, trust me, it works." She watched as his foot once again picked up speed. She put her hand on his knee, making him look at her. She met his eye. "Do you trust me?"

The redhead's gorgeous teal eyes became magnified as his eyes watered slightly before he blinked back the tears. "I trust you." His foot stopped tapping.

For a moment, Jordan thought as if he might hug her again, but Daisy bounded into the room before he could. "Okay, well, laptop or no laptop, I can still work on tracking Adley. Can I use your laptop, Jordan?"

"Of course, it's there on the table." Jordan pointed to the small kitchen table that was cluttered with the entirety of the mission file that had been spread about the surface.

Daisy grabbed Jordan's laptop and brought it over to the living area, sitting on the arm of the couch as she opened the laptop and typed in the password.

"You know, Jordan, you really should change that password."

"But then how would you get into all of my stuff?" Jordan teased.

"You know I'll figure out your new one." She nudged her partner with her foot. Pulling a small flash drive from her pocket and plugging it into the computer, Daisy brought up the tracking software that she had been using to locate Adley. When Jordan read about the watch design, she came across a feature of which none of them had been aware. Every Agent's watch comes fitted with a tracker, only to be used in case of emergency. This definitely was an appropriate time to use it.

"I've almost got the location pinned down. I've been narrowing it, slowly but surely. Certain building infrastructures can slow down the tracker; I'm assuming they're keeping him in one of those, that's why it's taking so long. I give it another couple of hours before we have his exact coordinates." The small girl smiled proudly.

"Good work, Daisy. We should all get some sleep; we're going to need it." Jordan got up from the couch, tightening her ponytail. Her hair was also very messy, as she thrashed a lot in her sleep, but her regular morning routine basically consisted of taking out the ponytail that she slept in and redoing it. If it were a good day, she'd brush it.

"Where is Daisy to sleep? She can have my bed if she likes, I can sleep out here on the couch. I doubt I'll sleep much, anyway." Dresden once again licked his palm and smoothed his hair down, becoming self-conscious after seeing Jordan fix her hair. Jordan noticed this, of course, but decided not to say anything.

"No, that's alright, she can sleep in my room with me." Jordan offered. "We've had to share a bed during a couple of ops before. You would think an Agent House would have more than one bed, but evidently not," she quipped, chuckling slightly. "Come on, guys; let's get some sleep." She looked at Dresden, who looked away sheepishly. They both knew that he wouldn't be sleeping tonight. She wished there was something that she could do to help him.

"Goodnight, Dresden."

"Goodnight, Jordan."

•   •   •

A few hours later, Jordan's alarm clock buzzed. Jordan smacked it into silence, allowing her eyes to flutter open, expecting to see Daisy's long black hair strewn against the pillow next to her, but she saw nothing. She bolted up, ignoring the headrush that caused colored spots to cloud her vision. "Daisy?" she shouted, bolting out of bed and running into the living room, where she saw Daisy on the couch, Jordan's laptop in her hands. Jordan breathed a sigh of relief.

"I woke up early and came to check on the tracking software." Daisy didn't look up from the computer.

Jordan nodded silently as if she hadn't just had a small heart attack. After a quick glance over at Dresden's door revealed that it was still closed, she walked back into her room and closed the door. She undressed, opening her closet and blindly picking one of her many black t-shirts. She pulled the shirt over her slight curves, but this was slightly difficult due to the bandage on her arm that she had now bled through. In addition to the bandage on her arm, she also had a brace around her midriff that she hadn't told the team about yet. She would have to get checked out at the Med Department again. After grabbing a pair of black jeans from her dresser, she slid on her shoulder holster and twirled her weapon into the holster that sat on her hip. She looked much like a movie poster with her holster exposed over her t-shirt. As she walked out the door, she grabbed her leather jacket and shrugged it on smoothly.

She once again glanced over at Dresden's room to see if he had yet emerged. When she saw that he hadn't, she walked to his door and knocked before cautiously turning the handle. She entered to see Dresden lying on his back, staring at the ceiling.

"Oh, hello," he muttered as she walked in.

"Dres, did you sleep at all?" The nickname felt oddly natural coming out of her mouth.

The redheaded Agent looked more disheveled than ever as he sat up, and Jordan already knew the answer to her question. "Yeah, me neither."

"What kept you up?" Dresden asked curiously.

Jordan shook her head. "Nothing, just thinking," she dodged the question. "Come on, let's go get Adley back."

•   •   •

Jordan strolled into Dresden's cubicle where Daisy had commandeered Jordan's laptop, and Dresden was twirling his cane nervously, as he usually was.

"Alright, I dropped the bag off to the Tech Department and explained the whole situation to them, and then I stopped by the Med Wing to get my stitches checked out. Apparently, I managed to rip out all of my stitches by thrashing in my sleep." Jordan slumped down in the unoccupied desk chair. "How's the tracking coming?"

"Nearly there. I should have it within the hour." Daisy remarked.

"What are we supposed to do until then?" Dresden asked, his cane picking up speed.

"I have to stop by the Mission Outfitting Department and pick up my jacket; it should be fixed by now. Do you want to tag along? We can train for a bit, that usually helps me get my mind off of things."

"Sure, I have nothing better to do." Dresden shrugged, continuing to twirl his cane as they walked out of the cubicle.

Daisy waited until the two had left before she stopped typing, reaching for her watch. "Mission Log One Dash Nine, Mission Code Name Masterpiece, February Sixth, Oh Nine Hundred thirty-three hours, Agent Daisy Muhuaná. I am very close to pinning down Agent Neilson's location, and we should be able to launch a rescue mission within the next couple of hours. Jordan and Dresden have gone to train for a bit in order to prepare and will return shortly. This is Agent Muhuaná, signing off."

•   •   •

Jordan walked out of the Mission Outfitting Department; her letter jacket draped over her shoulder. Dresden was standing outside the door, waiting for her so they could walk to the Training Wing.

"Daisy should have the location pinned down soon, but in the meantime, we can train." Jordan watched as Dresden carried his cane next to him.

"What type of training?"

Jordan paused to think for a moment. "I don't believe we ever got a chance to spar."

Dresden's oceanic eyes grew wider as he turned to Jordan. "Wait, what about your arm?"

Jordan shrugged. "I'll fight one handed. Maybe then you'll actually have a chance." She smiled at the redhead Agent.

"Are you sure it's a good idea to spar while you're injured?" Dresden sounded concerned, but Jordan only shrugged.

"Sounds to me like someone is scared to spar me." Jordan grinned.

Dresden chuckled. "We'll see about that."

The two of them walked toward the sparring mats in the center of the Training Wing, and Jordan stretched her muscles.

"Alright, let's do this." Jordan tilted her head to either side, popping her neck.

Dresden twirled his cane, stepping onto the mat.

"Hey, no weapons." Jordan pointed at his cane.

"It's only a cane," the tall Agent replied snidely.

"Nice try." She held out her hand, and Dresden sighed before tossing her the cane.

He watched as she gently tossed the cane to the corner of the mat. "Mercy rule?" he queried.

"Only if you think you need it, because I assure you I don't." Jordan smirked.

"I don't think I'll be the one needing it," he teased back.

Suddenly, Jordan leaped into action, her injured arm behind her back as she attempted to sweep his legs out from under him, but he jumped back. He threw a roundhouse kick at Jordan's ribs, but Jordan grabbed his ankle with her good arm and threw him backward. However, instead of landing on his back, he leaned into the throw, performing a back handspring. Jordan nodded. "Finally, a challenge for once," she muttered.

Dresden flashed her a charming smile before crouching down and throwing his leg out, attempting to trip her. Jordan sidestepped the attack, striking the Agent in the shoulder with a high-kick, wincing as the movement shook her ribs. Dresden stumbled backward but didn't fall. He grabbed Jordan's wrist as she threw another punch, turning and flipping her over his shoulder as if she weighed only two pounds. Jordan landed with a loud grunt of pain. "Ow." She swore under her breath, clutching her side.

Dresden appeared magically next to her, a bit of worry flashing across his face. "Sorry." He kneeled next to her. "Did you ever get that checked out?"

Jordan nodded. "Yeah, I'm okay. Only a couple of bruised ribs."

"Bruised ribs? And you want to *spar*? I thought you were intelligent, but this is dumber than the time that a drunk Adley put his shoe in the microwave."

Dresden held out his hand to Jordan, and she took it, standing up before gripping his arm and throwing him onto his back. "And *that* was dumber than letting a monkey steal your sunglasses."

Dresden popped back up immediately, seemingly unfazed. "Adley told you that?"

Jordan performed a no-handed cartwheel over the sidekick that Dresden attempted. "When you were taking your macaroons out of the oven." Her foot made contact with the back of Dresden's knee, causing him to lose balance and fall to the mat.

"Bugger," he mumbled, using his legs to propel himself into the air, landing back on his feet.

Jordan didn't skip a beat as she used a sidekick to the chest to knock Dresden off balance again.

The taller Agent stumbled back once again. He cartwheeled around Jordan until she had her back to him. Before she had the opportunity to turn around, he had already snaked his arms under her armpits, holding her head forward in a headlock. Jordan struggled, attempting to free herself, but the redhead's grip didn't weaken. She suddenly swooped low to the ground, the movement sending him flying over her.

Dresden dive-rolled onto the ground, once again expertly landing on his feet. "You're proving to be quite a worthy opponent, I must say. After what happened in the warehouse, well…"

Jordan side kicked him again, this time in the collarbone, causing him to fall onto his back.

"I would have thought you would have proved yourself inferior." He coughed, the air knocked out of his lungs.

"Just because I didn't want to fight back doesn't mean I couldn't have," Jordan said defensively, performing another handless cartwheel over Dresden as he lay on the ground, rolling onto the mat. Dresden saw this and attempted to scramble away, but Jordan quickly put him in a chokehold. "I just didn't want to hurt you," the blonde Agent muttered.

Dresden flailed, his long arms attempting to pry Jordan's arm from his neck as his legs kicked frantically. He coughed, attempting to breathe. After a few moments of flailing had done nothing to loosen the Agent's relentless grip, the lanky Agent tapped his hand on the mat three times. Jordan released him, and he rolled over, coughing.

"Are you alright?"

The larger Agent regained his breathing, attempting to stand. Jordan grabbed his arm and helped him to his feet. She hadn't meant to have that tight of a grip on his neck. After another round of coughing, Dresden nodded. "Just peachy."

"Sorry," Jordan muttered sheepishly.

"Just consider it payback for that bruise on your jaw." A pang of guilt struck Dresden. "I really am sorry about that. I don't know what came over me."

"It's alright; it's not like you were wrong. I definitely deserved it."

Dresden shook his head. "No, you didn't. I shouldn't have let my temper take control of me like that."

"Hey, it's okay, really. I've survived *much* worse than this," she teased, elbowing Dresden in the stomach lightly, but wincing when his countenance revealed she had struck a bruised spot. "Sorry."

"Does it hurt?" he asked, gesturing toward her ribcage.

"Only when I breathe," she muttered as they walked back to Dresden's cubicle, Jordan picking up Dresden's cane as they left.

CHAPTER TEN

Dresden and Jordan strolled into Dresden's cubicle, laughing.

"Right on time, I just pinned down the location. It seems they are holding him in an abandoned restaurant. It's only about fifteen minutes from here."

Jordan and Dresden's countenances changed immediately. "I can have us there in ten." Jordan pulled her car keys out of her pocket, twirling them on her finger. "Suit up."

Jordan grabbed several extra magazines for her pistol, storing them inside her jacket. Daisy took multiple spare knives, and Jordan saw Dresden fiddling with his cane, though she wasn't sure why. Jordan updated the mission log as they walked out the door.

"Mission Log One Dash Ten, Mission Code Name Masterpiece, February Sixth, Ten and Fifteen hours, Agent Jordan O'Connell. Agent Muhuaná has pinned down the location of Agent Neilson to an abandoned restaurant that's approximately ten minutes away. As of now, we are all prepared for an armed extraction mission and hope to recover Agent Neilson *today*, proceeding with the case directly after. This is Agent Jordan O'Connell, signing off."

Dresden lost count of how many red lights and stop signs Jordan ran on the way to the restaurant. He sat in the passenger seat of Jordan's sleek black car after Daisy had deferred to the backseat. Looking out of the window, he absorbed the blurry landscape as it whizzed by.

The '69 Chevelle looked like something straight out of the movies and much more at home in Hollywood than cruising down the dusty streets. Everything about the vehicle screamed efficiency: the crisp lines of the dark, shiny finish of the car, the chrome plating on it, and the meticulous cleanliness that characterized the whole vehicle.

As Jordan inched up on the location that Daisy found earlier that morning, the first thing that the team noticed was the overall air of neglect around the building. Two stories tall, the building was masked almost entirely by a thick blanket of ivy that wound its way around the chimney and the rungs of the rusty metal staircase leading to the top of the building. The grass around it almost covered the top of the very high ground floor windows, swaying as if it had a life of its own. If there was anyone in there, they did an admirable job of hiding it: the few windows on the top floor that were intact were clear of ivy and very obvious to any onlooker, but there was no sign of habitation even to Dresden's trained eyes. Jordan's eye, however, picked up on a small place on the glass where someone's finger had recently displaced a small patch of dirt.

"They're here," she muttered.

"How can you be sure? It seems to be deserted, judging by the amount of mortar crumbling off of the bricks and the distinct lack of a side door," Dresden commented, raising a fiery red eyebrow skeptically.

"Correction." Jordan walked up to the edge of the building, where she could see a small imprint in the overgrown grass. "The lack of an *obvious* side door." Jordan looked at the masonry, seeing that only one of the bricks was clear of lichen. Pressing it, she found that it easily gave way into the wall, causing a section of the wall to move, shedding dirt onto the ground and creating a doorway.

"Awesome!" Daisy bounced excitedly.

Jordan drew her gun, looking back at the others before taking point, Dresden directly behind her.

Suddenly, the grass rustled strangely behind her, and Jordan swung around to see Dresden ducking his head suddenly. "Get down; there's a sniper's perch on the top of the building adjacent to us."

Jordan swooped lower to the ground and quickly entered the building, the other two following behind her. She led them through the dark, twisting corridor, balancing her pistol on her left wrist, allowing her eyes to adjust to the darkness. A noise echoed off of the walls behind her, followed by muffled swearing and a stifled giggle. She turned around again to see Dresden crouching a little lower in the passage, gingerly rubbing his head, and Daisy with her hand covering her mouth. "These villains must be terribly short," he muttered.

"Or maybe you're just tall," Jordan retorted, turning back around and continuing down the dimly lit passage.

Jordan turned the corner, listening intently for footsteps. Her own footsteps were silent as she walked toward the door at the end of the hall. She looked back at Dresden, who put his hand on the doorknob. Jordan raised her gun, so it was pointed at the door, nodding at Dresden, who nodded back before flinging open the door. Jordan pointed her gun inside the room, two Agents standing at the other end of the chamber turning toward them. Two shots fired simultaneously, and both officers dropped. Jordan looked over at Dresden, who had his gun raised. Moving in exact sync, they nodded at each other and continued to the other end of the room. Dresden once again swung open the door, but instead of two Agents, there was only a single chair in the middle of the dingy off-white room. There was a man tied to the chair, and he looked up suddenly, startled at the door opening. It took a moment for them to realize that the man was actually Adley underneath all the mottled purple and black bruises and blood-stained clothes.

"Adley!" Dresden ran toward the chair, examining his partner's wounds. "Are you alright? What happened? What did they do?"

Adley smiled, but Dresden could tell that it was forced. "I'm alright, or would be if everyone here didn't have such abysmal wardrobe tastes."

"Glad to have you back, Adley." Jordan chuckled.

"Is someone going to untie me?" Adley raised an eyebrow.

Jordan pushed Daisy's jacket aside and pulled one of her knives out of its sheath, crossing over to Adley and cutting the ties around his arms. Adley rubbed his wrists as Jordan cut through the rest of the ropes. He took the knife from Jordan, flipping it around and holding it by the blade to give it back to Daisy. "The fearful dragon has brought a party on a quest to free the knight. Thank you, M'lady," he said dramatically, jumping out of the chair and into a deep bow. He winced at his own dramatics, as every small movement hurt due to his most recent encounter with Drina and her brass knuckles. He turned and hugged his fiancé, who quickly returned his embrace, not letting go for a few moments.

"Come on, let's get you out of here." Jordan still had her gun drawn, nervously glancing toward the door. Out of the corner of her eye, she heard a strange clicking sound and saw a flash of silver metal transferring from Dresden's hand to Adley's. She turned to see Dresden had unscrewed the globe from the top of his cane and had pulled out a sword, giving it to Adley. She thought back to the file she had seen the day before. *Adley Neilson; Weapon of Choice: Sword.* She smiled slightly, quite interested in how skilled the blond man would be with an actual weapon.

As if reading her mind, Adley appeared at her elbow. "Don't worry Miss Bond; I'm quite adept at using my oversized toothpick."

Jordan chuckled. "There are probably more Agents waiting outside the door; we should find another way out."

Adley's eyes fluttered over to the painting. "Does this look out of place to any of you?" he asked, gesturing to the artwork on the wall opposite the party.

Jordan noticed the scuff marks offset about an inch to the outside of the frame. "It looks like there used to be a different painting there, one slightly bigger."

Adley nodded. "And look at this color scheme. It doesn't go with the rest of the room at all. Not that any of it matches, though. There's just something off about it; I can't quite put my finger on it." If she hadn't spent so much time with the secretary recently, Jordan would have sworn that he was being sarcastic. Still…

Jordan squinted at the painting. "A few drops of the paint are on the frame, and there's no signature anywhere. It's been painted over."

Adley smiled a bit, despite the obvious pain it brought him. "My thoughts exactly, Miss Bond."

He walked over to the wall, his eyes scanning the 'masterpiece' behind the dark bruises dotting his fair skin. "I'm not quite sure how Guano did it, but there should be something behind here…" he mused, curling his fingers around the dark wood of the frame.

"Guano? As in bat droppings?" Daisy asked curiously.

"It's a long story." Adley pulled the painting off the wall, and suddenly, a woman clothed in a periwinkle business suit flew out of the tunnel behind it, grabbing blindly for his throat, but missing and falling to the ground.

"Don't badmouth me, you fat frog!" the woman yelled, her voice hoarse.

Jordan pointed her gun at the woman, keeping her in place. "Is this Guano?"

Adley nodded, kicking his former captor in the stomach as he moved away from her failed attack. "Also known as *kõhnmadu*."

"Skinny snake?" Jordan raised an eyebrow.

Suddenly, there was a bang as the door flew open, and about seven black-clad Agents stormed into the room. More began pouring from the passage that had been hidden by the painting, filling the room in moments. At a rough count, Jordan estimated there were at least fifteen Agents, if not more.

Jordan and Dresden pressed their backs against each other; their pistols held out in front of them. Jordan immediately took out two of the Agents that raised their weapons at her and Dresden. Dresden raised his weapon at one of the Agents aiming his gun at Adley, but Adley sliced through him with his sword before he could fire. Adley stabbed a couple more Agents as they went for Daisy, who had already lodged one of her throwing knives into the stomach of one of the Agents and pulled out another one of the fine blades.

Nine. Jordan kept count of the Agents. She heard a gunshot from behind her and turned to see Dresden falling to the ground, his leg bleeding from a gunshot wound. A string of swear words flowed from his lips under his breath as he put pressure on his wound with his hand. Jordan swore loudly, shooting Dresden's attacker in the head.

She dove behind the ratty couch for cover, grabbing Dresden's wrist and dragging him behind her. Adley grabbed Daisy and pulled her behind the couch with the others. Jordan handed Adley her gun as she took Dresden's jacket off and tied it around his calf, now gushing blood.

Suddenly, Jordan felt something cold on her neck. She gasped as she felt a hand on her arm drag her upward, a blade against her throat. She didn't have to see her captor to know that it was Guano. The other three turned to her, and Dresden instantly pointed his gun at the woman from his place on the ground, but didn't fire as the other Agents crossed over to their end of the room and trained their guns on Daisy, Adley, and himself. Jordan felt the edge of the knife press harder against her windpipe, and she held her breath, afraid to breathe. The villain turned her attention to Adley, who was staring at her with a burning hatred, his fingers wrapped around his sword. Drina jerked Jordan in her grip, positioning her so that none of them had a clear shot without having to go through their teammate. At the sudden movement, Jordan flinched, inhaling sharply.

"You and this knife are good friends, no? Why don't I introduce your friend here?" She slid the blade across Jordan's throat like a deadly caress, not enough pressure to cut the skin. "After all, its encounter with one blonde wasn't enough. We need a little bit more of an—" Drina lowered her voice and hissed the words in Jordan's ear—"*intimate acquaintance.*"

Jordan gulped, the lump grazing against the knife. She looked down at Dresden, whose face seemed frozen in a look of horror, and she suddenly flashed back to the warehouse. She had to get him to look at her, but saying his name would compromise him. She thought for a moment.

"Seven." Jordan tried her best to sound militaristic, but she heard her voice tremble. Dresden met Jordan's eye in surprise. She looked into Dresden's oceanic eyes, mouthing the words carefully as she tried not to move her head.

Take the shot.

Dresden paused, his gaze flickering from Jordan to Drina, to the blade pressed against Jordan's throat, before slowly setting down his gun, his hands rising from his sides and climbing into the air in surrender. Guano cackled loudly in Jordan's ear when she spied Daisy and Adley following suit. The other Agents lowered their weapons after a nod from Drina.

What is he doing?

"You sniveling busybodies! Too much emotion, not enough *method*." She grinned wickedly as Daisy turned to face her, hate and fear clearly warring with each other across her face. She looked at Dresden, still sitting on the ground. "Get up," she spat.

"He's injured," Jordan snapped through gritted teeth. The woman pressed the knife harder against her throat, silencing her.

Dresden looked at Jordan, nodding to tell her it was alright. Adley offered his hand to help him, but he pushed it away and stood, putting less pressure on his bleeding leg, raising his head in defiance as Jordan did in the warehouse.

Drina grinned. "Now, you've given me another victim. I'll have to sharpen my little friend: It got rusted with all the sugar in the veins of the blond cow. Hopefully, you'll be a bit more cooperative, or I'm afraid you will end up worse than your friend."

"Do your worst, Guano," Jordan hissed.

"Oh, I will," Drina remarked snidely, raising the blade from Jordan's chin up to her cheek, abruptly slicing the skin along her cheekbone, making a very deep cut before roughly kicking Jordan in the back of the knee. A small cry escaped Jordan's lips. "Walk to the door, and maybe I'll keep you alive for that much longer."

"You better go ahead and kill me; you won't get anything out of me." Jordan straightened up again and raised her chin as blood dripped down it, the blade returning to her throat. She refused to move; her feet planted on the ground. Drina looked up to see that the other three members of Jordan's team had their weapons out of reach before lowering her knife to Jordan's shoulder, slowly and deliberately dragging the blade through the skin all the way down to her wrist. Jordan saw Dresden's hands ball into fists as she winced in pain but stood her ground, her feet like anchors, keeping her in place.

"You're just as stupid as your fat little friend." The serpent behind her sneered, punching Jordan in the throat, causing her to collapse. She sprawled out on the carpet.

"That's enough!" Dresden shouted, his nails digging into his palms.

The woman raised her eyebrow as she kneeled next to Jordan, who kicked at her assailant as she walked toward her. Drina jumped backward, and Jordan scrambled to her feet. The others looked over to the Agents training their guns on the three of them, ready to fire if they moved toward their boss.

Jordan's gaze flickered between her team, the other Agents, and Drina, who grinned.

"Let me remind you that my men will fire on your team if you so much as think of trying to run." Drina grinned, walking toward Jordan.

Jordan glared at the woman but didn't move away. "Do what you want with me, leave them out of it."

"As you wish." Drina punched Jordan in the face, kicking her to the floor. Jordan opened her mouth to check if her jaw was still in one piece, not moving away when Drina knelt next to her, lightly dragging her blade down Jordan's thigh before suddenly plunging it into the muscle. Jordan bit her lip to keep from crying out as her eyes watered.

The woman yanked Jordan up by her gashed arm, causing a small yelp to escape from her.

The shorter woman grabbed her arm and spun her around so that she had Jordan's arm extended behind her back. Jordan's face contorted in pain, having to shift all of her weight onto her good leg.

"Stop it!" Daisy screamed, her voice scratchy and raw.

"What do you want?" Dresden asked frantically.

"What do I want? Hmm…" Drina pretended to think for a moment, staring off into the distance before a sudden movement drove the knife into Jordan's forearm. Jordan screamed, squeezing her eyes shut, not wanting to look any of her teammates in the eye. Daisy lunged forward, but Drina had already twirled Jordan back to her, once again allowing the cold metal to press against her throat. Adley grabbed the small Agent, not allowing her to lunge at Drina, his own face a mirror of the girl he was holding by the arm. Horror flashed across his face, imagining Drina inflicting the pain he had gone through on Jordan. He realized suddenly that the pain would be worse, as he knew Jordan would never break against Drina's blade.

Jordan struggled against the woman, but she simply put more pressure on the blade, giving one small sudden movement the ability to split her windpipe.

Drina locked eyes with Dresden, the burning hatred in his eyes fierier than his hair. The woman's voice really did sound like a snake hissing in her ear. "I want you to watch your friend *Jordan* here suffer."

"That's not my name," Jordan growled, the sharpness of her voice slicing through the air around her.

Drina rolled her eyes obnoxiously. "Her name will be the least important information I will cut out of her." She sneered. "And I will have all of the time I need, because this time, there won't be a rescue mission, because if you try anything, I will kill her." Drina's voice was terrifyingly gentle, making Jordan shiver slightly.

Dresden's gaze flickered to Jordan, who finally met his eye. He felt something inside him snap as he looked into his teammate—his friend's—brown eyes, filled with unshed tears.

"If I go with you, how do I know you won't hurt my team?" Jordan spoke roughly, her voice like gravel.

"If you come with me now, I won't need your team. They will be free to go once my men and I leave the premises." Drina grinned.

Jordan couldn't bring herself to meet the eyes of anyone else on her team.

"Now walk," the snake woman demanded, shoving Jordan toward the door. The other Agents were still waiting for their boss to give the all clear to fire again if anyone so much as moved. Jordan finally succumbed, still unable to look her team in the eye, dragging her feet toward the exit, but still raising her chin, a mask of defiance over her. She stood tall, even with the pain from every step shooting through her leg, forcing her tears to finally spill over, pouring down her face.

"You won't get anything out of me, you know," Jordan growled, her teeth clenched.

"We'll see about that." The dark-skinned woman kept the knife on Jordan's throat as they turned toward the exit, but they never got there. There was a strangled cry mingled with a gunshot, and a loud clunk as a body fell to the floor. The bullet buried itself in the back of Drina's head, almost in slow motion. The blade fell from Jordan's throat.

Dresden was blowing on the muzzle of his gun with a look of red-hot fury on his face. "I never was good at close-range shots with handguns, but I suppose I see better from a distance." He stalked toward the corpse of Drina with a clear purpose and the manner of a caged tiger despite the bullet buried in his calf, delivering a vicious kick to the dead woman's side, but clearly regretting it as he winced in pain. "I can't stand narcissists," he muttered.

Jordan fell to one knee, using her hand as support so she wouldn't put pressure on her leg which had now bled through her jeans. The knife had managed to tear a rather large hole in the denim. She coughed and pressed a hand against her throat as Dresden appeared at her side. "I'm so sorry, I couldn't take the shot with you in the way, I couldn't risk that. I had no idea she would do that to you." He placed a hand on her shoulder. "Are you alright?"

Jordan nodded, attempting to stand, but not entirely succeeding, and she leaned on Dresden for support. She met his eye as he held her, and he saw that her tears had spilled over, despite her efforts. She looked up, wondering why the Agents hadn't fired yet when she saw the rest of Drina's Agents lying at the feet of Adley and Daisy, who had their blades drawn, dripping blood on the terrible carpet. Adley crossed over to Drina's corpse, plucking his navy blue pocket square from her blazer pocket.

Dresden handed Jordan her pistol, and she smiled slightly before wincing as more blood dripped down her face. She placed the gun in her holster, inhaling sharply as she bent her arm.

"Let's get out of here." Dresden nodded to the others. Jordan and Dresden used each other as support as they walked out the door.

CHAPTER ELEVEN

Three of the four Agents were sitting in Dresden's cubicle once again, Adley was sitting next to Daisy on Dresden's desk, each holding a colorful pen. Dresden, now sporting a cloth bandage over his stitches, looked over to see that Adley had turned his scabbed-over wounds into several tic-tac-toe boards, and was attempting to beat Daisy.

"I really wish you wouldn't do that. You're going to reopen those wounds," Dresden said worriedly, shooting a meaningful glance at his partner.

"But I'm so close to winning, Con-Man. One game won't hurt," Adley whined, sticking his bottom lip out in a pout like a three-year-old.

Dresden sighed. "Fine, just be careful." He paused. "Did you ever stop by the Med Department?" He had been released after his partner, as it took longer to remove the bullet from his calf.

Adley nodded. "Yes, they cleared me. They said the bruises should clear up soon, but there aren't any signs of internal bleeding, just external." He winked at Dresden. His bruises had mostly cleared up already, but part of his face was still swollen.

"You seem to have taken that rather well," Jordan spoke up from the doorway of the cubicle.

Dresden shot up out of his chair before he was quickly reminded of the stitches in his leg. "What did they say?"

Jordan shrugged but immediately regretted the action. She had three small white pieces of tape on her cheekbone, holding together the gash which had finally stopped bleeding. She was still wearing her letterman jacket, even though it had been ripped every which way from Drina's blade. "They gave me a few stitches; I'm alright. I'm supposed to rest until I get the stitches removed since I reopened all of my old ones again. I guess I won't get to spar you two anytime soon." She smiled at Dresden and Adley. She turned to the smaller man. "You seem to be holding up well."

"Well, of course, dah-ling. I knew what I was getting myself into." Adley made another mark on his arm.

Jordan looked up. Dresden stopped fidgeting. Daisy stopped writing.

"What?" They all asked simultaneously.

"Oh come on, you don't *really* think I would let myself get captured if it wasn't purposeful, do you?" Adley looked around at the shocked faces of his teammates. "Wow, I'm hurt. You all have no faith in me, and I'm Gold, too." He crossed his arms in mock offense.

"You had me worried bloody sick, and you're saying you did that on *purpose*? You could have been killed, or worse. Jordan nearly *died* trying to bloody rescue you! Why would you do something so stupid?" Dresden's face was a mixture of anger and con-fusion as he berated his partner.

"To get information, of course. Guano gave me quite a bit of it, and I have it all recorded." Adley smirked, marking another move on his arm. He paused, looking up at Jordan. "I really am sorry about what happened to you, both of you, if I had known..."

Jordan shook her head. "It's alright, I've been through much worse. I must say, I underestimated you, Neilson."

"Now why would a girl as smart as yourself do such a thing?" Adley asked teasingly.

"In our defense, Daisy and I didn't know that you were Gold until the Director told me. Well, and I looked at your file," Jordan pointed out.

"Wait, the Director granted you access to my file?" Now it was Adley's turn to look shocked. "I feel violated."

"Well, we were trying to save you. So yes, I looked at your file. Pretty impressive, I must say. But I was the only one who had access; I just asked Daisy if she knew that you were Gold." Jordan shrugged.

"Why didn't you tell us?" Daisy asked, drawing a line across Adley's arm, indi-cating she had gotten three in a row.

"Well, to be quite frank, I thought Miss Bond would be able to deduce it," Adley said honestly, bringing a hand up to his mouth and spitting on it, then rubbing vig-orously at his neck. He continued to talk: "With all the fabulous deductions she was making, I thought for certain she'd notice that my foundation shade doesn't quite match my skin, and I was hiding something." He moved his hand and revealed a very detailed rose tattoo that wound up the right side of his neck.

"Of course I noticed, I just assumed you were covering up a birthmark or a scar or something, I didn't think it was that important." Jordan's voice trailed off as she crossed her arms over her chest. "I just didn't know your code name until I had access to your full file. If I had access to it before, I would have known. Silver levels don't get code names," she pointed out. "So, Rosie, huh? What's the story behind that?"

Adley fiddled with his collar. "Well, I've always been a bit of a flower child, and roses are my favorite to paint. Training to be an Agent, Dresden was obviously very observant, and he gave me a rose on our first date. Further in our relationship, it was like our trademark, so I decided to make it mine in a literal sense."

"Using a pre-existing character trait for a codename is the exact same level of brilliance I'd expect from someone who microwaved a shoe," Jordan teased.

Adley looked at Dresden. "You told her about that?"

Dresden snickered. "Maybe…"

"Consider it payback for all of the embarrassing stories you told me about him." Jordan grinned.

"Plenty more where that came from, love." Adley winked at her.

"I think the Director wanted to see us once Adley and Jordan got checked out. We should update the mission log first, though." Daisy spoke up from the corner, placing her pen back in the cup of rainbow ink.

"A capital idea!" Adley beamed, sliding off the desk to sit next to his fiancé. "Who will do the honors? Miss Bond?"

"I think you should do it," Jordan responded. "You were captive, after all. You should update them on the status of your wounds."

"Alright, if you insist." Adley flipped his long ponytail off of his shoulder and pressed the button on the side of his watch. "Mission Log One Dash Eleven, Mission Code Name Masterpiece, February Sixth, Fifteen Hundred hours, Agent Adley Neilson. I have been rescued from captivity by the fabulous Agents Daisy, Jordan, and of course, Dresden. We also recovered the painting, which was hidden in plain sight in front of me, the prisoner of war. Why criminals have to be more extra than the chewing gum brand, I have no idea, but once the first layer of paint was scraped off, it revealed the missing artwork of old and crusty fighting men, so all's well that ends well. Obviously, I'm not dead, and we await the congratulations dinner, which better have macaroons. Ta ta, this is Agent Neilson, signing off."

"'Old and crusty fighting men.'" Jordan quoted lightly. "You know that was a Revolutionary War painting, right? It depicted—"

"I know, dah-ling, I know. I just wanted to mess with the history nerd of the group." He winked at her again, and she rolled her eyes.

"How about you two go ahead and stop by Evidence Department and check on the painting before heading to the Director's Office?" Dresden asked hopefully. "You can lecture Daisy on it as much as you want."

"Nice try, Dres. We're going to see the Director together. Come on." Jordan chuckled playfully, strolling out of the cubicle, the other three in tow.

Dresden huffed. "Coming, coming." He picked up his cane and trudged after them, obviously dejected.

As the foursome walked down the hall, Adley slipped back to his partner's side, grabbing his hand. "Come along, slowpoke. We're going to be late," he said cheerfully.

CHAPTER TWELVE

They all stood in front of the Director's desk, Jordan and Daisy on one side, Dresden and Adley on the other, with Dresden and Jordan standing next to each other in the middle. Dresden was tapping his foot nervously, and Jordan shot him a look. His foot stilled.

"Good work, all of you. It has come to my attention that not only did you recover Agent Neilson, but you also recovered the stolen painting. I also heard that Agent Neilson obtained some inside information during his time as a captive."

Adley nodded. "Yes, sir, the woman who was interrogating me said that the art theft had just been a cover-up in order to capture an Agent. She also mentioned something about the 'CFH,' whatever that is. The full audio recording is on my watch, unlike my blade, which is not on there." Dresden elbowed Adley in the side.

"Did you give up any information?" the Director asked, ignoring both Adley's comment and Dresden's elbowing.

Adley shook his head. "No sir, but there was something that she already knew." The others looked over to the stout Agent. "She knew Jordan's name."

The Director arched an eyebrow, shooting Jordan a concerned look. "How?"

"She heard Daisy yell it when Jordan was shot." Adley laughed, although it wasn't entirely appropriate. "That's why I called her Guano: she claimed to be called 'Bats' for her super hearing, but to me, she was a load of—"

"That's enough, Agent Neilson." The Director held up his hand. "You all went above and beyond to rescue Agent Neilson. Something I would expect from Agent Connors, of course, but I must say, you two surprised me." He turned to Jordan and Daisy.

"Agent Neilson is one of our own, and he's an excellent Agent, sir. We would have stopped at nothing to get him back." Jordan stood up straighter, if that were possible, and shot Adley an appreciative look.

"Yes, I am aware. I'm glad to see that my original hunch about the four of you was correct. You all work very well together, I must say. That being said…" The Director turned to Jordan and pulled something out of his desk drawer. "Congratulations, Agent O'Connell, as a result of exemplary work on this mission, your evaluation has been conducted, and you have been promoted to Alpha-Nine. You are now a Gold Level Agent." He handed Jordan an Agent ID card, the same as the one she currently had, except this one said *Alpha-Nine* on it and had a gold insignia rather than a silver one.

Jordan took the card, running her finger over it as the gold letters caught the light. "Thank you, sir," she said breathlessly.

"You've earned it, Agent O'Connell. I heard you were involved in two hostage situations on this mission. Not only the one involving Agent Neilson but one involving yourself. You subjected yourself to the possibility of death or worse to protect your team. You told Agent Connors to take the shot, even though it was almost certain that you could have been killed. That shows real resolve." The man nodded.

"I had faith in my team, sir." She smiled, meeting his eye again.

"Of course, now that you're a Gold Level, you'll need a code name." The Director began to type on his desktop.

Jordan looked over at Adley. She paused for a moment. "Bond," she said finally, grinning at Adley, who returned the gesture.

The Director arched an eyebrow. "Bond?"

Adley nodded. "Of course. It does fit her, you know."

"I suppose you always did have a flair for the dramatic, Miss Bond." The Director smiled.

Jordan shrugged. "Maybe just a little."

"I have something for you as well, Agent Muhuaná." The man opened his desk drawer, pulling out a hot pink laptop. "The Agents over at the Tech Department were able to recover the hard drive, and all of your data has been transferred onto this new laptop."

Daisy's face lit up, taking the laptop as he handed it to her. "Thank you, sir."

"As for the two of you—" He turned to Dresden and Adley, snapping their attention back to him. "Well, you've both proved yourself on this mission. I am hereby reinstating Agent Neilson as Agent Connors' partner."

Adley and Dresden looked at each other, grinning from ear to ear. "There is one condition," the Director held up his hand. The two froze. "You are now a dual pair team." He pointed at Jordan and Daisy. "With them. If you'd like, of course."

"Yes!" the four of them exclaimed simultaneously, causing the Director to grin.

"I suspected as much. When you've recovered, there are plenty of dual pair missions to assign."

"We've recovered enough, sir. We're ready whenever you need us." Jordan raised her chin.

"You say that every mission, Miss Bond. Take a few days to recover. That's not a request." He met Jordan's eye, but she didn't look away.

"Yes, sir. Thank you, sir."

"You're free to go." The Director gestured toward the door. Jordan nodded toward him respectfully before strolling out of the office, the others following.

•   •   •

They were all sitting in Dresden's cubicle once again, Jordan admiring her new ID badge.

"You know what this means." Adley looked over her shoulder at the ID badge. "You're the youngest Agent ever to reach Gold Level."

Jordan swiveled around in the desk chair. "Really?"

Adley nodded. "I held the previous record, and I was twenty-seven when I reached Gold, right before I stepped down."

"So I beat your record?" She grinned slyly.

"Don't get too cocky, Miss Bond. I'm still the superior." He winked again.

Jordan chuckled. "Our little sparring match says otherwise." She pressed the button on the side of her watch. "Mission Log One Dash Twelve, Mission Code Name Masterpiece, February Sixth, Sixteen Hundred hours, Agent Jordan O'Connell. I have been promoted to rank Alpha-Nine, courtesy of the Director. Agent Muhuaná has also gotten a new laptop, but the biggest development is that Agent Neilson has been reinstated as Agent Connors' partner, and the Director has now made us a dual pair team." She looked up at Dresden, smiling widely. "This is Agent Jordan O'Connell, signing off."

CHAPTER THIRTEEN

Jordan once again walked up the stairs of the posh housing development to Dresden and Adley's penthouse, but this time, Daisy was with her. Jordan knocked on the door before turning the handle and strolling inside.

"It's me!" Jordan shouted into the apartment, closing the door behind her and leading Daisy through the winding hallways into the conjoined kitchen/dining room/living area.

"Oh, I'm so relieved. See, I thought it was a serial killer," Dresden yelled back from his post next to the stove. He turned around and gave Daisy a rare smile before going off to find Adley. "Is the knight done finding the Holy Grail?"

Adley suddenly appeared next to Jordan, once again wearing an entirely new suit. This one was a dark plum, his periwinkle tie and pocket square standing out starkly against the white button-down underneath the purple blazer. He seemed to have finally found the boots with the fringe, as he was wearing them, and they were every bit as impractical as they sounded. He had a paintbrush behind his ear and seemed rather preoccupied, but instantly broke into a grin when he saw Jordan.

His hands were behind his back, and a mischievous grin plastered on his face. "The knight has evaded capture!" he crowed, then sank into a bow. "The dragon and the knight have a present for you, for lending your aid to the dragon as he was having a hard time with my absence."

He proffered a rather bulky package wrapped in primrose-colored tissue paper and tied with a golden ribbon. "Be careful; it is a fragile relic."

Jordan untied the ribbon with a single pull of one end, carefully removing the tissue from around the package. The corners of her lips turned upwards into a smile, even though the gesture caused pain to shoot through her cheek. She turned to Dresden, who had appeared next to Adley as she was opening the gift.

She held in her hands a vase that was originally white but was now mostly covered in color. The scene was a beach with peach-colored sand dotted with flowers next to a deep lake. Dominating most of the painting was a flaming red dragon whose tail was curled around a cane with a small skull on top of it. Sitting on the scarlet coils of the dragon's tail was a knight whose armor seemed to be slightly rusty, and his helmet was topped with a peacock feather. He held his helmet in his hand, letting a blond ponytail flow down his back. At his feet, the lake faded gradually from a clear blue that matched his breastplate adorned with a rose to a greenish hue, a mermaid holding a hot pink laptop and sporting a flower crown drifting in the tranquil water. Her dark hair rippled in the water behind her.

In the forefront of the vase painting, there was a blonde woman with a gun drawn dressed in shining chain mail and with a knowing smirk on her face. Underneath the picture, Adley had written in flowing golden script *Adley the Knight Requires Assistance.*

Jordan placed the vase on the table and abruptly wrapped her arms around Dresden, who grunted in surprise but quickly hugged her back. She quickly pulled away, surprised at her sudden outburst of emotion. Her cheeks had flushed under the bandages that covered one of them.

"This was your idea?" she asked Dresden.

Dresden smiled. "Yes, but Adley's the one who painted it."

"Thank you." Jordan turned to Adley. "Both of you."

Adley bowed deeply. "You're very welcome, Miss Bond."

"Dinner's almost ready, have a seat." Dresden gestured to the dining table, where four places were already set. Jordan and Daisy sat on one side of the table, and Adley sat on the other, leaving the empty spot next to him for Dresden.

Dresden returned from the kitchen, placing a serving plate overflowing with shrimp fettuccine alfredo on the table, as well as a large bowl of salad and a smaller plate of homemade bread. He looked like a fancy waiter, balancing so many plates and bowls on his arms.

Jordan immediately took two helpings of salad and drizzled some vinaigrette over it before taking some of the pasta and two pieces of bread. She quickly dug into the salad while the others were serving themselves.

Adley poured himself a glass of wine, deciding not to mock Jordan again as he saw her holster peeking out from under her leather jacket.

Daisy took a bite of her pasta, her eyes lighting up. "Dresden, this is incredible!"

Dresden smiled, his cheeks turning a slight shade of red. "Thank you."

"I told you he was an amazing cook." Jordan nudged her partner in the side.

Dresden suddenly became very interested in his plate, moving his pasta around with his fork. Jordan nudged his foot under the table. "Just wait until you taste his baking."

The four of them ate and told stories, Jordan telling the story of beating Dresden in their sparring match, and Daisy attempting to retaliate with an embarrassing story about Jordan before Jordan quickly changed the subject. They all sat at the table long after they had finished their meal, telling stories and laughing. Finally, Dresden took their plates back to the kitchen, and they all went to sit on the couch. The laughing stopped for a moment, and Adley took the opportunity.

"Um, Jordan? I wanted to tell you something…"

Jordan stopped, sensing the seriousness in his voice. She looked over to Dresden, but he was nowhere to be found. "What is it?" she asked cautiously.

"Well, Dres told me about what happened when he was at your house, and how he found some medication…"

"He told you about that?" Jordan's voice was more concerned than angry.

Daisy looked up at Jordan in surprise. "Wait, what?"

Jordan placed her hand on Daisy's knee. "I didn't tell you about that yet… I'm sorry, I was planning on telling you later."

Adley nodded. "Yes, he told me."

"Oh." Jordan looked down at her hands in her lap.

"Don't worry; we're all here for you." Adley smiled warmly, looking up at the taller Agent.

"All of us," Dresden spoke from behind the couch, causing Jordan to jump.

Jordan smiled, looking down again. "Thanks, guys. I really appreciate it."

Dresden walked around to the front of the couch, holding a platter of macaroons. "Anytime, Miss Bond." Dresden smiled, handing her a macaroon.

"How are your injuries doing?" Adley asked, motioning to his arm with a pen to catch Daisy's eye before Dresden noticed.

"Oh, they're doing alright," Jordan muttered, her hand defensively running over her jacket sleeve as she ate her macaroon.

"Can we see them?" Dresden asked, snatching the pen from Adley before he and Daisy could start another game of tic-tac-toe. The blond pouted but quickly pulled out yet another pen, still keeping his eyes on Jordan.

"Oh, um, I don't think that's a good idea…"

"We just want to see how well they're healing," Adley insisted.

"I told you, I'm *fine*. Why do you want to see my wounds so badly?"

"Because they're probably a lot worse than you're letting on," Dresden said honestly.

"Come on, just let us see," Adley whined.

"I really don't think—" Jordan was too late, though, and Dresden had already rolled up her sleeve, despite her extreme resistance. There were several cuts along her arm from Guano, and her arms were red and raw from the blade. Among the new cuts, however, were a series of older scars. Jordan quickly snapped her arm back from the others, rolling down her sleeve again.

The others sat in silence for a moment. "Jordan…" Dresden began sheepishly. "What are those other scars from?"

Jordan shook her head. "Just, another mission. I got captured. It's no big deal."

Daisy looked up at Jordan. "Jordan, you can tell them."

Jordan shook her head violently as if she could shake the thoughts loose.

Dresden gently put a hand on her shoulder. "That is far too regular in size, shape, and diameter to be anything like what Guano did. I'm sorry for playing Sherlock Holmes this time, but I'd much rather have heard it from you. Tell as much as you feel comfortable about, but don't keep it to yourself. *Please*."

Jordan exhaled shakily, placing her face in her hands. She drew her knees to her chest. Muffled within the ball of her own solitude, she began to speak. "I was at a low, okay? It was high school; I was being bullied by everyone; constantly told I wasn't good enough. I was told so often; I realized it was true. I thought maybe I should punish myself somehow, punish myself for not being good enough. So, I did." Her voice was shaking, and it sounded like she was having a hard time breathing.

"But we've seen you without your jacket before, and we never saw them," Adley queried.

"You're not the only one who knows how to use concealer," Jordan mumbled. "I might not wear makeup on my face, but I know how to use it."

Dresden pushed Adley off the couch and sat next to Jordan, placing two fingers under her chin, attempting to lift her head to make her look at him. She resisted.

"Look, we're not going to make fun of you or take pride in your pain. This isn't like that; you're not alone and battling everyone's hate. We're not on the same level of those vermin who hurt you, damn it, we're your *friends*. We're here for you, and we're not going anywhere, I promise." Dresden's own voice was shaking now, desperately attempting to get Jordan to look at him.

Jordan finally gave in, allowing him to lift her head toward him. When he did, he saw that her cheeks were now wet with tears. His shoulders dropped, and he pulled

Jordan into a tight hug. Softly, his British accent making her think of the time at her apartment, Dresden said, "Oh, Jordan, you're not alone anymore."

Jordan allowed Dresden to pull her tighter as more tears began to roll down her face, the salt stinging her open wound, but she didn't care. "I just wanted to be the strongest, so I could prove myself to everyone who called me weak. But they were right."

"Hey, listen, you're one of the strongest people that I know. I could never do *half* of the things you do. You were willing to be captured and tortured just to protect us. That takes a special type of strength. One that not many of us possess. You've done something with your life, you've risen up out of oppression. You've made all of us proud, and have become the youngest Gold Agent. So many people can't do *anything useful at all*, and here you are, being brave, strong, and—" he blushed a little— "a beautiful human being."

Jordan burrowed further into Dresden's arms, and Dresden hugged the blonde Agent so tight he was afraid he might break her ribs. "Thank you," he heard her mumble through the tears that were now staining his shirt.

Dresden looked up to see Daisy holding Jordan's hand. She met his eye. "You knew?" He silently mouthed the words. Daisy nodded, tightly squeezing Jordan's hand.

"I'm sorry," Jordan mumbled. "I'm such a baby, I know."

"Hey, don't do that. Having emotions doesn't make you weak, it's what makes you strong. Suppressing your feelings never ends well. We're all here for you, Jordan. You can tell us anything." Dresden wiped away the tears from Jordan's cheeks, and she winced slightly as he ran his finger over the cut on her face, and he quickly pulled his hand back.

"I'm here for you too, you know." Jordan looked up at Dresden.

Dresden paused for a moment. "There's something I want to tell you."

Jordan met his eye. "You know you can tell me anything." She wiped her tears and pulled away from Dresden's hug, trying to gather herself again.

Dresden awkwardly perched on the edge of the sofa, not meeting Jordan's eye as he tried to gather his thoughts. "Well, ah, I—" he swallowed hard, his face going pale as he squeezed his eyes shut to avoid looking at the rest of his team. "Jordan, I wasn't entirely honest with you about my terrible backstory as I didn't mention some crucial points. It didn't seem important at the time, but since we're going to be a dual team now, I suppose I'll have to tell you all sooner or later." He took a deep breath and stiffened his grip on the arm of the couch, his knuckles draining of color, making him seem much more vulnerable. Adley appeared at his fiancé's side, putting a hand on his shoulder and giving a reassuring squeeze. Dresden continued. "I played off my anxiety problem, and it's crucial for this dual partnership to work out. Ah, you see, I am *terrified* of people. Scared to death of new things, new faces, things I don't understand. I can't deal with them; they're all too special, too wrapped up in their little lives to notice when others are falling apart. It makes me sick, and I can't help but look out at the world and feel fear: Who's going to take away my money, my almost nonexistent self-worth, my fiancé, my family—" he paused, and it seemed like he would melt into a puddle. Adley made a sympathetic clicking noise with his tongue and enfolded his partner into a tight embrace. Dresden continued, although a little muffled, "One day, I can't stop something terrible from happening, and the underlying brutality of life will take over the sunshine and rainbows. I can count the people that I trust on one hand, and they're all sitting in this room.

"That's why I go abroad so often; I can get the cold water treatment: perilous situations, unknown environment, strange people, everything on edge. Living in a life of doubt helps you forget the doubt that lives inside."

"Dresden," Jordan placed a hand on his arm, "we're not going anywhere. Nothing is going to take us from you."

Dresden shook his head. "I saw you with Drina. You were willing to die for us. And at that moment… I realized that I wouldn't know what to do without you. Our line of work is one of the deadliest, and that's what makes it so tough; your best friend could be the corpse you stumble over tomorrow."

"I've proven myself on more than a few occasions to be a tough girl to kill." Jordan smirked. "I'm not going anywhere. I'll always be here, I promise."

"So will I." Daisy nodded from the other side of Jordan.

Dresden slowly got up from the couch, an expression of doubt written across his face.

Adley pointed to his engagement band. "And I'm afraid you're stuck with me," he teased, standing on tiptoe to give Dresden a peck on the cheek.

"What if you all get tired of me, like everyone else?" Dresden muttered; his cheeks red from the kiss.

"Then that would be a real shame, considering we're a team now, and definitely stuck together for a while," Jordan teased. She watched Dresden's facial expression, still unconvinced. "Dres, we're not going to get tired of you. You're stuck with me. Especially because now you know about my issues and if you weren't my friend anymore, I'd have to kill you to keep that secret."

Dresden snorted. "It's not me you have to worry about, Adley'll blab about anything."

Jordan pushed her jacket aside, pulling out her pistol. "Then we might have a problem." She winked at Adley.

"Hey, hey! I'm not a violent kind of guy. Last time I shot someone for no good reason, the blood wouldn't come out of my suit, and now I have a bloodstained white suit."

"Not a violent guy? You sliced through nine Agents earlier." Jordan chuckled.

"That was different; I did it to protect you." Adley pouted. He paused for a minute, watching Jordan twirl her pistol around her fingers. "I won't tell a soul, I promise."

"Good." Jordan returned her gun to her holster. "Because if you did, a blood-stained suit would be the *least* of your concerns."

Adley rolled his eyes, but still looked relieved when she put the weapon away. "Now that you've stopped this nonsense, I dug up the Monopoly board. I have a winning streak almost as good as Dres' sniper record, and I intend to keep it."

"Oh, you're on." Jordan grinned, grabbing the plate of macaroons as Adley set up the board.

•   •   •

Several hours, murder attempts, death threats, tears of rage, and a small macaroon fight later, King Adley was standing on top of the Monopoly board with a cardboard crown and sword, one foot lightly resting on Dresden's head as Daisy threw money at the ecstatic Agent. "Peasants! I won all your dollars!"

"All hail King Neilson!" Daisy shouted, allowing more of the paper money to rain down on Adley.

Dresden rolled his eyes. "One, you stole half of my money when you hit me in the head with a macaroon, and two, if you don't move your foot, the ferocious dragon will come back to life and bite it."

Adley stuck his tongue out at Dresden but moved his foot. "Well, I beat you, Miss Bond." Jordan, who had her gun sitting in her lap, craned her neck up to meet the gaze of the portly Agent standing on the table.

"Um, I don't think cheating counts, which makes me the rightful winner." She smirked.

"I didn't cheat; you can't prove it, anyway," Adley said snidely.

"I saw you snatch a fresh stack of twenties from the bank when Dresden threw the macaroon back at you and hit Daisy instead," Jordan said matter-of-factly.

"Well, okay, so maybe I did," he admitted, before drawing back up to his full height. "But you are a *peasant*. You can't stop the King."

Jordan pulled her gun out of her lap and lazily pointed it at Adley. "The 'King' is wearing a cardboard crown he hastily stapled together in the last round."

Adley made a small squeak and dropped down on the table, landing on Dresden. "Killing off your opponents is also cheating, Miss Bond."

"No, it's only leveling the playing field. I—" Jordan stopped, jumping suddenly.

"What? What's wrong?" Dresden turned to Jordan.

"Are you guys not getting that?" Adley asked.

"Getting what?" Daisy queried.

"It's a code message from the watch. I thought only teams could send messages to each other, though," Jordan wondered out loud.

"The Director can send a message to anyone," Daisy pointed out.

Dresden shoved Adley off, rolling into a sitting position and looking at Jordan with interest. "What does it say?"

"I'll translate it." Adley pulled out his pen.

"It's a mission briefing," Jordan interrupted him.

"How did you—" Adley began. "Right, eidetic memory. I forgot."

"We have a new mission. Code name Camouflage. Report as soon as is convenient. Mission location: London," Jordan said as each word came through.

"Oh, the mother country! How exciting!" Adley nudged Dresden playfully.

"I was born in the States, you twit." Dresden rolled his eyes but smiled anyway.

Jordan grinned and pressed a button on the side of her watch. "Mission Log One Dash Thirteen, Mission Code Name Masterpiece. February Sixth, Twenty-Three hundred hours, Agent Jordan O'Connell. The team has just received a new mission, Code Name Camouflage, so this will be the last log for this mission. The Director seems to have been right with his hunch about the four of us, as we appear to be getting along quite well." Jordan winked at Adley.

"We *were* until Jordan accused me of cheating!" Adley shouted from where he had been pushed onto the floor.

"And until Adley threw a macaroon at me," Dresden added.

"And Jordan threatened to kill Adley," Daisy pointed out.

"Hey, he threatened me first!" Jordan exclaimed defensively. She chuckled. "Anyway, this is Agent Jordan O'Connell,"

"And Agent Adley Neilson!"

"And Agent Daisy Muhuaná."

"And Agent Dresden Connors."

"Signing off," the four of them finished at once.

ABOUT THE AUTHORS

Sam and Allison are two best friends currently in high school, who have been writing for nearly their whole lives. Having met in the third grade and reuniting in ninth, there is never a dull moment between the two.

www.ingramcontent.com/pod-product-compliance
Lightning Source LLC
Chambersburg PA
CBHW061747050726
47598CB00002B/615